CAPE MAY GHOST STORIES

David J. Seibold   Charles J. Adams III

EXETER HOUSE BOOKS
Barnegat Light, N.J. & Reading, Pa.

CAPE MAY GHOST STORIES
by David J. Seibold and Charles J. Adams III

Exeter House Books
PO Box 6411
Reading, PA 19610
www.ExeterHouseBooks.com

ISBN **978-0-9610008-7-5**
First Printing, 1988
THIS EDITION COPYRIGHT 2007

Printed in the United States of America

TABLE OF CONTENTS

INTRODUCTION

This is our second book dealing with the "other side" of life along the Jersey Shore.

In themselves, they are not remarkable. Many have written about the supernatural as it pertains to Garden State towns, countryside and beaches. Stephen Crane's series on New Jersey ghosts included several accounts of spirits and ghouls that made the 19th century reader shiver with a demented delight.

Crane, best known to the populace for his "Red Badge of Courage," produced volumes of tales of terror in New Jersey while writing for a New York newspaper and one story, that of a ghostly black dog, has some ties to Cape May.

In the story, the unfortunate animal was washed ashore on a shipwreck, presumably along Long Beach Island. Its master died in the wreck, and his body was protected on the beach by the dog.

A band of salvagers, or more correctly "wreckers," as they were known in those days, happened upon the wreck and sought to pilfer anything they could.

The faithful dog growled at the intruders as they rifled the wreck and stripped the dead bodies of any personal valuables. When they approached the dog's "best friend," it reared up, bared its teeth and lashed out to protect the corpse.

The ruthless wreckers were undaunted. One of them grabbed an ax, twisted it over his shoulder and plunged it into the head of the dog.

As Crane said in his chilling piece, the spirit of this black dog still roams the New Jersey coastline. "There is a dreadful hatchet wound in the animal's head," he wrote, "and from it the phantom blood bubbles. His jaws drip angry foam and his eyes are lit with crimson fire."

Is Crane's story fictional?

Does it matter?

There may or may not be any relation between Crane's ghostly dog and another strange occurrence along the Cape May beach several years ago. No fiery eyes were seen and no hatchet wound was noted, but then again, the person who saw what she saw that evening in September, 1980, chose not to look too closely.

The young woman from Staten Island, N.Y., chose to remain anonymous. She feared that having her name published in a book would bring her ridicule and embarrassment. While the credibility of the story may suffer a bit because of it, the story is nonetheless true.

She said she was walking the beach alone on a misty night the week after Labor Day, 1980. She said she prefers the beach resorts then, and always rents a small home in Cape May Point during that time.

It was twilight, but still bright enough to easily recognize the distinctive form of the Cape May Light a few hundred yards up the beach. The light fog reduced visibility to, in her estimation, a couple of miles.

"Never in my life have I believed in ghosts or horror movies or anything like that," she said. "Really, I never went to horror movies or read anything scarier than Charles Dickens. I guess I lead a rather boring life, generally, so what happened that night was a big deal for me and really stands out in my memory."

The statuesque woman, a computer programmer for a large company in Manhattan, stressed the fact that she was never prone to believing in ghosts or recognizing that things like monsters might exist. "I either laughed or paid no attention to those stories of things like the Loch Ness Monster, Bigfoot and others," she said.

"After what I saw down at the Point that night, though, I might have to think again. Maybe these people who say they have seen these things aren't crazy. I know I'm not, or at least I don't think I am!

"There's not much to it, really," she continued. "All I know is that I was walking by myself that night along the beach and I saw a black dog come out of the ocean. Now, does that sound strange, or what?

"There's really no other way to put it. I only wish my girlfriend had been with me. She laughs about it whenever I bring it up, and she always rides me about it. She asks if I've seen any dogs come out of the ocean every time I say something a little strange. I guess I never should have told her about it.

"Anyway, I was walking along the path through the dunes, and when I got to the ocean side, I just kind of stood there for a few minutes and looked out at sea. The waves were crashing in, and my eyes just kind of fixed on one place in the surf.

"I was watching for quite a while, I mean, a couple of minutes at least, when I thought I saw something bobbing around in the waves. At first, I thought it was someone in a wetsuit. It was black, you know, and that's what it looked like.

"Well, within a second or so it was very obvious that it was a dog. It was a fairly large dog, but it was all wet, of course, so I couldn't really tell what kind of dog it was.

"It just seemed to walk out of the waves. It didn't seem to be tossed around or anything, it just walked right out with no problem. Well, at first, I only thought that it was a little strange. Then, though, I realized that, my gosh, I was watching that general area of the surf for a few minutes and I never saw any dog go into the waves. How the heck did it get in and where the heck was it coming from?

"I did a double-take and tried to reason out what I saw. This damned dog just seemed to walk out of the ocean waves. I couldn't figure it out.

"One thing I remember that may be a little silly, but the dog didn't shake off the water. You know, most dogs, as soon as they get wet, shake off. This one didn't. It just came straight toward me, and I figured I'd better get out of there. The dog was very real, as far as I could determine, and who knows what it might do.

"So, I hustled back over the dunes, looking over my shoulder every couple of steps. One time I looked back to see where the dog got to, it wasn't there.

"I'm not saying I saw a monster, or that the dog was supernatural or that it disappeared. I'm only telling you what I saw, and that it scared the heck out of me, and I'll never be able to explain it to myself rationally."

It wasn't until after the woman related her story to the authors that they discovered the Stephen Crane writings. When the woman was contacted again and told of Crane's ghostly black dog legend, she recoiled in shock and amazement.

Such stories of the unexplained help to enrich an area's heritage. Many people are reluctant to admit to the possible existence of spirits or unnatural creatures, and refuse to even divulge experiences they themselves have had.

Still, there are many who have added stories to the ledger of legends on Cape May and beyond. Author Larona Homer did so in the fine "The Shore Ghosts and Other Stories of New Jersey" (Middle Atlantic Press, 1981) and singer-storyteller Jim Albertson preserved many colorful legends on the superb album, "Down Jersey: Songs and

Stories of Southern New Jersey" (Folkways Records, 1985).

By far, New Jersey's most recognizable "monster" has been, for centuries, the Jersey Devil.

There is a professional hockey team that pays tribute to the legend of this monster from the Pine Barrens. A shop at the Historic Towne of Smithville sells Jersey Devil souvenirs. Indeed, the Stone Harbor Golf Club was once called the Jersey Devil Country Club.

Has this most lofty of legends ever set its cloven hoof on Cape May soil? Some say yes.

James F. McCloy and Ray Miller, Jr., in their definitive book on the Jersey Devil, entitled, "The Jersey Devil" (Middle Atlantic Press, 1976), indicate that the monster was spotted once in the Cape May County village of Burleigh.

Nora T. Vivian, in a 1963 article in the Philadelphia Bulletin, detailed the story of the Jersey Devil and wrote, "The town of Burleigh in Cape May County reported frequent visits from the Jersey Devil, who on one occasion left his tracks in the snow and on the porch roofs."

The creature, as best determined, was the 13th child born to a Colonial-era Leeds Point woman. She cursed it upon its birth, causing it to take on various horrible configurations and wreck havoc in New Jersey and points just west of the Delaware.

Cape May native Jim Keltie doesn't particularly believe that the Jersey Devil ever really existed, but he relates the strange story of "Puss" Williams, whose coon dogs were once scared to submission by something "out in the country" of rural Cape May County.

Williams was a stocky fellow who often went into forest and field with his two fearless coon dogs. He bragged that they weren't afraid of anything.

One day, however, the dogs and Puss himself met their match. They were treading through a wooded area when the dogs began to bark incessantly, charging toward their prey.

Puss Williams headed along the trail they were leading and all of a sudden, something big and black—that's the only way Puss or Jim Keltie could describe it—something big and black popped up in front of the hunter.

At once, the dogs ceased their barking, began to yap, and turned tails back to Williams' home. The confused Puss Williams did the same.

Puss never could describe what he saw that day, and he said it took him a good two days to convince his big, brave coon dogs to come out of hiding under the front porch!

A more credible story was told by the Rev. Albert V. Lang, in one of his popular "Fish Tales by Cap'n Al" columns in the Cape May County Gazette several years ago.

Under the heading of "The Sea Lizard," the fishing minister wrote of a bizarre creature caught by a woman off the Cape May coast. It was described as being about three to four feet long, with the tail and legs of an alligator and a blunt snout.

The creature reportedly began to bite the boat it was hauled onto and thrashed about wildly as its captors attempted to subdue it. Finally, the skipper of the fishing boat clubbed it to death in a frenzied battle.

Back on land, an incident at a Cape May County campground still has twins James and Jeffrey Seyler of Shillington, Pennsylvania, befuddled.

The two teenagers remember the incident well, and claim that others could readily verify everything they told.

"We were down at the shore one night camping," James says. "It was the middle of the night, about ten after three, and this thing was howling. It was no dog, no animal, it was screeching and then howling. Then, we heard hooves, or the sound of something running.

"It woke up the whole side of the campground. Some people thought it was a mule, some thought it was a horse or a pig, or a wild boar chasing a deer.

"It was a horrible scream, and while it was going on, there were no crickets, no sounds of the forest. It was very scary."

James Seyler says the strange silence continued for about a half hour until the crickets and more docile night sounds resumed.

Jeffrey says some people claimed to have seen hoof marks in the dirt near where the sound came from, and those familiar with the Jersey Devil legend claimed that it could very well have been a visit from that elusive and seemingly immortal beast.

IS CAPE MAY HAUNTED?

The title of this chapter is a question the authors have tried for more than a year to answer.

Perhaps there is no clear cut answer. Perhaps there are no such things as ghosts at all, and "haunting," in a spectral sense, is the figment of man's collective imagination.

Cape May *looks* haunted. The tangle of streets in Cape May city, the lonesome roads of the upper cape, and the hidden beaches of the bay are among the features that lend themselves to ghostly goings-on.

The stately Victorian homes and inns, each with its own legacy, seem so inviting for ghostly tales that it then seems inevitable that fleshing out the fleshless beings that are sure to walk their corridors would be an easy task.

Not so.

At times, the search for Cape May Ghost Stories led to resistance, ridicule and disappointment. There were several valid leads, but more often than not these turned into what could be classified as "they say" ghost stories. "They" say that a particular building is haunted, and "they" have had experiences in it. But the "they" could never be found and the tales were never documented.

Thus, there are several very prominent buildings of Cape May which have been omitted from this book. "They" said the buildings were haunted, but by whom or what remained a mystery because "they" remained a mystery.

This book is not intended to be a history book. Nor is it a testimonial to the positive presence of ghosts that walk just on the other side of our accepted reality.

The authors have written similar books in the Pennsylvania Dutch Country and on Long Beach Island, New Jersey. Legends and ghost stories abound in these areas, and in both cases the books have become accepted companions to the region's more traditional history and social studies.

If nothing else, this book on Cape May Ghost Stories should serve as the kind of volume you keep around for rainy nights when it's a little darker than usual. Or, it could be reading fodder for the beach. You could lose yourself in its intriguing tales and try to capture some of the rich lore that makes Cape May a very special place.

There is a very important word in the book's title. These are Cape May Ghost *Stories*. Just *stories*. There is no claim that any are necessarily tales of encounters with ghosts.

Still, it is difficult to disbelieve the words of the Cape May people who did come forth with their encounters with the unknown.

For reasons the authors understand and respect, some names in some of the stories have been changed. Some exact addresses of locations have not been revealed. But many of the stories, and their tellers, are readily identifiable.

ONE SUCH PERSON who is not at all hesitant to admit to a brush with what she believes to be a ghost is Jeanette Harris, of Stinson Lane, West Cape May.

The old home was built in the last century, and has housed generations of the Harris family. It is one of those ancestors Jeanette believes still remains in the house, years after his death.

Both Jeanette and her daughter, Christy, have had separate experiences in the old home. Both believe the presence there is that of Jeanette's grandfather.

She called him "Granddad," and it was in that house that he fell and broke his hip several years ago. He was taken to the hospital and never returned to the house in which he was raised and in which he had lived for all his life.

"I have a very good feeling about this house," Jeanette says, "and I cannot believe that whatever might be in here with us would not be harmless."

The former school teacher says she never particularly believed in ghosts, but always liked to read and tell good "spook" stories. It wasn't until her own experiences played out in the house along the lonely road in West Cape May that she began to feel that there might be something to those kinds of stories.

It was a quiet evening in the Harris home, with Jeanette preparing a meal at the kitchen stove. To her left, a staircase led to the second floor. She felt that someone was looking over her shoulder.

She slowly turned her head toward the stairway, and her eyes were led to the top of the steps. To her shock, there was the figure of a man standing there!

"It wasn't a solid figure," she recalls, "I couldn't make out any facial features. But it was dressed in work clothes and boots. My immediate reaction was that it was my grandfather. He was a farmer, and that's the way he would have been dressed."

Jeanette was swept with an avalanche of emotions ranging from fear to confusion to warmth. She feared that there might have been another unwanted person in the house. But within a millisecond, that fear turned to awe and a certain amount of love when she told herself it was the spirit of her dead grandfather.

As if to check her own vision, she turned away for an instant, and looked back to the top of the steps. The figure had vanished.

"I was really confused," she admits. "My first reaction was 'what is this?' 'Am I supposed to be scared?' 'Am I seeing things?' "

She lived with the experience for a long time without telling anyone, for fear of ridicule.

One day, however, she told her daughter of her isolated and unexplained sighting. Christy was dumbstruck.

It seems that Christy, too, had a similar experience in her bedroom on the second floor. She, too, had believed the apparition was benevolent, and probably a deceased family member.

One time, Christy was watching television in the parlor when she felt a very clear breeze and saw the very clear figure of a man brushing past her. She gave it no thought, believing that it was her father. The figure disappeared around a corner, and Christy wanted to say something to her father, so she got up from her chair and peeked around that corner to talk to him. He was not there.

When she finally caught up with her father, he was far away in the yard, and swore he hadn't been in the parlor for quite some time.

On a recent summer day, Jeanette had another strange thing happen to her. Again, she was downstairs and had the nerve-teasing feeling that there was someone else in the house with her. She knew, however, that she was alone.

She ventured close to the stairway, and believed that someone was lurking at the top of the steps. All along, she felt no fear, just the somewhat comforting feeling that perhaps it really was her grandfather's spirit that cohabited her home.

She looked up to the top of the steps. She noticed that a pair of cats had already been staring toward the second floor.

In a sudden fit of boldness, she called out: "Granddad—is that you? If you are there, give me a sign!"

The quote may not be exact. Jeanette admits that she was a bit flustered at the time. Regardless, she cautiously ascended the stairs and ventured into Christy's room.

She noticed that a closet door which should be closed was open. She gently pushed it until it clicked shut. She turned away and listened with amazement as the door clicked again and slowly creaked open.

Even more cautiously this time, she took the door knob and pushed it until the latch was securely and undeniably locked. She backed away, keeping her eyes on the latch, and was satisfied that it was closed.

Confidently, she turned away from the latch, only to listen with a tinge of goosebumps as it seemingly opened itself again and allowed the door to once again swing on its hinges.

All around her, in that upstairs room, virtually anything that could move began to. One of Christy's necklaces, draped over a post, started to swing, as did an assortment of ribbons, stuffed toys and other items that were hanging or suspended in any way.

Jeanette swears that there was no open window, no fan or vent. The swaying continued briefly with no apparent source of propulsion.

She watched in amazement, and finally resigned herself to the supposition that the energy within Christy's bedroom was that of her dead grandfather. After all, that room was his room when he lived in the house!

Exasperated and amazed, but again not particularly frightened, Jeanette simply spoke, to no visible listener, "All right, granddad, if you want that door open, that's fine."

The swaying stopped.

THE LOVELY HOMES in and around Cape May sometimes gain mysterious nicknames and reputations. One house in Cape May Point, just off the picturesque dunes, is called the "Gray Ghost."

The monicker may suggest the supernatural, but it is generally believed that the house is not haunted. It got its nickname because of its imposing gray hulk that looms in the fog and mist of the beach front.

Not only the homes, the inns, hotels and lighthouse of the cape have their legends. An old elephant had a tale, too.

It was a strange sight, this huge pachyderm that stood near the beach on land which was to become the town of South Cape May.

The development was the dream of real estate promoter Mark Devine, who used the elephant as a publicity gimmick. The wooden beast, called "The Light of Asia" or, more popularly, "Old Jumbo," was one of three along the eastern seaboard. Another on Coney Island is long gone, and only "Lucy," in Margate, N.J., survives.

The wooden elephant of Cape May survived fewer than twenty years, and the real estate Camelot of South Cape May stood for one, brief, shining moment before a savage storm swept Devine's dream to sea.

In 1900, the elephant was standing on shaky and sandy ground. The waves were threatening its stability, and it was demolished.

According to the affable former school teacher and Cape May historian, Sue Leaming, there is a persistent rumor that the pieces of the elephant were saved during the dismantling and were stored in a Cape May barn or warehouse. They have never been found, if indeed they were ever salvaged.

An even more tantalizing rumor about "Old Jumbo" is that it was haunted.

As newspapers were wont to do in the last century, a pathetically small and teasing article in a Cape May paper stated that the "wooden elephant is said to be haunted. Strange sights and unearthly voices are of nightly occurrence."

It could be that pranksters were causing the ruckus, and unenlightened passersby were spooked. But then again. . .

IN WEST CAPE MAY is a fine structure that may very well contain the remnants of a 17th century whaler's quarters.

Located on the former Fow Tract, the house has been known as the Fow House. More recently, it was the Swallows Restaurant.

Bob Guldin and Dan Ness now own the building, and do not disallow the possibility of a spirit or two in the old place.

One corner of the building is said to be a tiny whalers cottage dating to the late 1600s. There is some indication that the two-story cottage was moved to the site from Town Bank.

The house served as a railroad depot, and a Red Cross station during its existence.

Guldin says the grave of a Frenchman was discovered several years ago in the yard of the Fow House. The body was estimated to be from the early 1700s, and there is a theory that it may have been the remains of a pirate ship crewman.

No treasures have turned up in the yard, but a brass Spanish hinge was found on the property.

Guldin has many stories about the old house, including one regarding the late Madam Regar, who owned the home for much of the 20th century.

It was believed that the woman horded gold coins, and visitors to the place reported hearing the glanging of coins and the slow counting sound of a woman's voice coming from the second floor from time to time.

No ghostly counting or coin jingling has been heard, but some former employees of the Swallows say they scratched their heads in amazement more than once as unexplainable incidents played out before their eyes.

Barry Marron, who was a partner in the restaurant business, admitted that some ghostly occurrences took place in the five years he was involved in the business. Most of the reports came from waiters and waitresses.

One woman told the story of a Catholic priest, a regular customer in the restaurant, who was sitting at a corner table in the oldest section of the structure. He was enjoying his favorite dessert, a strawberry served in a glass. With no warning, and for no apparent reason, the glass shattered. He hadn't touched it, but as the waitress said, "it just exploded in front of him!"

On another occasion, the same priest, seated at the same table, was engaged in after-dinner conversation with friends when a glass lamp shattered before them.

The priest took it with good humor, but the staff members who watched the incidents or heard about them later preferred to be wary of what might have caused the inexplicable breakage.

Those who worked in the Swallows say they felt comfortable with whatever might have "haunted" the restaurant, but most of them say they have had their own brushes with the unknown and unexplainable in the building. Napkins fell from tables with no breeze, footsteps could be heard where no feet were, and icy chills could be felt in the warmth of the kitchen. In all, as one waitress said, the ghost, if there is any, was "mischievous."

CAPE MAY BUSINESSWOMAN Jeannie Kosak tells the stories of two Cape May properties she has owned that she believes are haunted.

In order to protect the present owners of the buildings, we shall refer to Kosak's former residences in generalities. One is in the 1000 block of Washington Street, and the other is in the 800 block of the same street.

Of the property in the 1000 block, Kosak says, "My first realization that something was the matter was that I got two telephone calls, one after the other. They both were from tenants in the building saying that there was a big crash in the main part of the house, which was empty. I went down, there was nothing there.

"Both tenants reported the sound of a mirror falling off a wall, or something like a big chest of drawers falling over and glass breaking. But the room was totally empty."

There were subsequent calls from the tenants, reporting much the same noise. Even Kosak's daughter, who lived in the apartment building, heard it.

"My daughter and her husband were absolutely terrified by it," Kosak says. "They would hear somebody walk up the steps very distinctly and go up to the door on the landing. They could hear very heavy breathing for awhile, and then it would just stop.

"Then, they said they'd actually hear and sometimes see the doorknob to that apartment turn. Then, they'd hear the heavy breathing again. That happened all the time. As long as I owned that property, I could never keep a second-floor tenant."

Ms. Kosak says she has often felt the presence of something in the 1000 block of Washington Street building. She further states that she felt it represented "fear and evilness."

She says she once saw a shadowy figure pass by her on the second floor landing just seconds before she, too, heard the footsteps coming up the steps. She heard them plainly, but saw nothing.

Jeannie tried on several occasions to exorcise the spirit from the house, but the disembodied footsteps, shadowy specters and unexplained sounds persisted.

"I think the scariest was that there were many times I would awaken very abruptly because I absolutely knew there was someone in the room," she says. "Of course, I'd look around and I was alone."

Jeannie Kosak had moved into the place after others had heard the strange sounds, and continued to live there for four years until she sold the property. In the course of her research on the house, she did discover that there was once a suicide committed on the second floor landing of the central section—exactly where the footsteps had been heard and the shadowy figure had been seen.

When she sold the property recently, she warned the incoming owners of the strange occurrences over the years. They said they would cope with them.

"I've never regretted selling it," Jeannie says. "The new owners have done a lot of nice things to the place, and it really is beautiful. But I really believe it is haunted.

The other home, in the 800 block of Washington Street, is one of those fine old whaler's homes of Cape May. If Jeannie Kosak's experiences are any indication, that house, too, is haunted.

"The house had two stairways," she says. "At the very top of the back steps, one time, I felt a chill. That was no big deal. But my husband had an experience in that house. He actually heard what he described as a family in the empty parlor, laughing, eating, with pots and pans and dishes clanking, et cetera, as if it was a family at breakfast.

"He heard it while he was at the top of the steps. He said it was very plain and definitely coming from the bottom of the stairs.

"As he cautiously went down the stairs, the sound faded away and eventually ceased."

The Kosaks' children say they detected another spirit

on the third floor of the building. "We called it an 'afternoon ghost.' You would hear the rustling and crinkling of taffeta as the ghost of a woman ascended the steps, almost every afternoon. You got so used to her, and the other strange sounds, you just co-existed with them.

"The children would often complain about another weird and sorrowful sound in the house," she continues. "They said it was the sound of a young girl crying. It was a very soft cry, but they could tell it was somewhere in their room, and it was a little girl."

ONE OF THE STATELY BEACHFRONT INNS of Cape May, the "Colvmns By The Sea," (which utilizes the Roman "U" in its logo), has also had its share of the unexplained happen within its walls.

The elegant B & B on Beach Drive was built in 1905 as a summer "cottage" for a Philadelphia dermatologist and his family. In the 1940s, new owners converted the building into an apartment house, and in 1984 the 20-room building was renovated into an inn by Cathy and Barry Rein.

Its red and white shutters gaze across the boulevard and beach to the open sea. Waves crash over the sea walls and tickle the Colvmns with spray as seagulls squawk their haunting, lilting melodies overhead.

And perhaps, just perhaps, spirits dwell within the rooms of the old Victorian cottage.

We return to Bob Guldin, of the Fow House, for an experience he had at the Colvmns. "I have heard and even seen several things I couldn't explain at the Colvmns," he says. "I heard a very plaintive sigh downstairs one time, as if someone was sitting next to me, but there was nobody there. Another time, I heard the sound of people shuffling around on the floors upstairs, but again, there was nobody up there.

"Another time, I looked into one of the guest rooms and saw a figure on the bed. The next morning, there was also an imprint on the bed as if someone had slept on it. Of course, there was nobody really there."

Or at least that's what Bob would like to believe!

The Reins love their inn. They took a long time, a lot of money and put a lot of love into their restoration. Victorian antiques and Chinese ivory carvings today grace the public areas of the inn, and the entire building is elegantly appointed.

Both of the two major unexplained events the Reins report occurred during the extensive renovations.

"In the main parlor," Barry says, "there was a beveled mirror. As we were working on the house, we noticed that the mirror was surrounded by moisture. We checked, couldn't find any leaks. My carpenter, who is perhaps on the superstitious side, said the house must be crying, because it is being restored. We checked all over and found no leaks or any possible source of the moisture."

There was a similar problem on an interior wall of the staircase that leads from the parlor to the second floor. Moisture kept appearing, but there was no piping nearby and no plausible explanation.

There are some vague notions, buried deep in the lore of the house, that the spirit of a woman does indeed linger there. Nothing further could be found on that legend, but the Reins seem comfortable with it.

Cathy and Barry say there have been several other isolated incidents on the second floor. An old wicker baby carriage in the hallway has moved on its own, and guests reported the doors of the upstairs suite—the former master bedroom—have opened and closed without anyone being near.

Actually, the carpenter's theory on the house "crying" because it was undergoing renovations does not stray far from one very well accepted and interesting "explanation" for the existences of ghosts.

To most people who collect ghost stories, the basis for the existence of the spirits borders on the scientific.

In the vast majority of cases, ghostly occurrences take place in buildings that are in the process of, or have recently been renovated.

It has been speculated by some researchers that the physical disturbance of the structure may very well release the psychic information that is "stored" within it.

The hypothesis is relatively simple, and entirely reasonable.

Medical science has ascertained that the human body contains a certain amount of electrical energy of a sort. It charges our nerves and fires our brain. In its own way, it is a very powerful force.

Some believe that at the time of extreme stress or trauma, some of this human electricity is discharged from the body. There need not be a death, but any great shock on the individual involved might spark the release.

In the case of death, however, it does not necessarily have to be violent. Thus, the common perception that "ghosts" are the products of violent deaths could be considered flawed.

At the time of the release of this energy, it is further theorized that bits of the electrical impulses could explode into the atmosphere of a building and find a medium. On this medium, then, the impulses actually deposit or record.

That medium, it is felt, could very well be rust. Similar to the recording of sound waves onto tape in the tape recording process, these waves of human emotion, imagination, intelligence and memory remain bound on ferrous oxide.

As with a tape cassette or reel, the recording is useless without a "playback" device.

That is where the psychic or medium comes into play. Such a person, gifted (or cursed) with the ability to "read" houses and identify presences receives the messages from the deposits on the rust.

These shards of information are "played back" through the medium, and the "picture" of an important event that caused great impact on a human life in the building is painted through the psychic process.

Obviously, the renovation or rebuilding of a structure reveals many ancient features, rusty nails, etc., which could harbor these "messages." As the building's walls and floorboards are ripped apart or exposed, the recorded information is more easily accessible.

Unsuspecting residents or guests in the building—people who have had no brush with the psychic phenomena and no knowledge of their own level of psychic awareness—suddenly "play back" the long-hidden bits and pieces of a person's life.

That, then, becomes a ghost. That psychic image becomes an apparition when the frail and impressionable human imagination takes over and conjures up a vision of the subject of the recording. It is similar to a simple exercise any of us can try.

When told to imagine, say, the president of the United States, certain images come immediately to mind. Facial features, hair styles and stature are easily retrieved through memory. The imagination enhances these images, and the individual is clothed, colorized and maybe even animated.

Much the same can take place through the audible sense, when sounds can be attached to the psychic "recordings." And, physical movements can be created by more intense energy that is stored within walls, ceilings, floors or stairways. Thus, objects can move for no apparent reason.

The theory can sound outrageous to some. But then again, a century ago, the notion of recording a symphony on a thin strip of rust-coated plastic would have been equally laughable.

THE GHOST OF WINDWARD HOUSE

The doors to the Windward House are magnificent. Massive planks of oak and chestnut frame meticulously-crafted beveled and stained glass panels. The inn itself is a spectacular presentation indicative of the refined tastes of its proprietors, Sandy and Owen Miller.

There is a very real possibility that the Windward House is also haunted.

It is not an appealing proposition for many innkeepers in Cape May (or anywhere) to handle. Many people shy from or totally deny any speculation that their home or place of business may be inhabited by unseen tenants.

Indeed, when the authors began serious research into the ghost stories of Cape May, they were tersely and firmly advised by one woman that they'd not find ghosts in Cape May. "Ghosts don't fit the image of Cape May," was the curt reply to the quest.

Further probing, interviewing and random questioning resulted in a much more enlightened view on the possibility of ghostly occurrences in Cape May town and county.

Owen and Sandy Miller have no qualms about admitting that their charming inn might be host to a ghost. They have put their love and a great part of their lives into the Windward House, and its opulence reflects that fact.

The public rooms of the inn at 24 Jackson Street in Cape May are veritable museums of the Millers' zeal for collecting things like egg cups, Edwardian and Victorian furniture and accessories, and vintage Victorian womens' wear.

The guest rooms, each with its own name and theme, are large and inviting, and furnished with a superb collection of antique furnishings, fixtures and fineries. Most include a small refrigerator and ceiling fans. Some are air conditioned, but sea breezes waft through most rooms, keeping the machines idle a great deal of the time.

In all, the Windward House is a superb place to stay. And, if various guests are to be believed, one former resident chose to stay in the old house for an eternity.

Known in historical circles as the George Baum House, the building was erected as a summer home for a Philadelphia lawyer in 1905. It became a rooming house in the 1940s, after a colorful existence as a private residence.

Some say the rooms on the third floor of the house were once the servants' quarters, where a staff of Irish immigrant women lived. Some even say one of them may never have left.

Every tone, every color and blend of human drama has doubtlessly been played out within the walls of the Windward House. As so many more of the large and small hotels and inns of Cape May, it seems to have a personality of its own. The streets of Cape May's central area seem to breathe with history and the real and imagined ghosts of those who have walked there before seem to float on the sidewalks and whisper just behind the next tree or around the next corner.

As for the Windward House, its resident ghost may be as close as the Wicker Room on the third floor.

Sandy Miller is open and, in a sense, welcoming when the talk turns ghostly. "One senses," she says, "that there was much happiness here."

Those who claim to have had supernatural experiences in the Windward House over the years feel that same feeling of contentment, even with the spectral resident.

Just who has seen or felt the presence at the Windward House? Sandy, a statuesque, stunning woman, and Owen, a man who looks for all the world to be exactly what he is, the keeper of an Edwardian inn, both say the witnesses to the ghostly events have been many.

"The second year we had the house, in about 1978," Sandy recalls, "we were newcomers to the business. We had never slept in any of the guest rooms, and we'd never had any supernatural experiences, as such.

"We had a gentleman stay with us one summer for a couple of days. He was very delightful. He told us he was back in graduate school taking a course in English. He stayed for the first time in July and came back later that summer, in August.

"At that time, he requested the same room, which surprised us because it was not our most popular room. It was a room on the third floor that shared a bath, was not on the ocean side of the house, and was a very hot room."

In fairness to the Millers and anyone contemplating a stay in the "haunted" room, this "Wicker Room," as it is now known, has been air conditioned and redecorated.

Back to Sandy Miller's story: "After he stayed that second time, on his way out he said, 'I have to tell you something. Believe it or not,' he said, 'I'm writing a paper for a graduate course I'm taking and I wanted to include a story about your house.' He said he had a particular reason for writing it. He was convinced that we had a ghost!"

There is only a slight pause, a puzzled curling of the lips and arch of the eyebrows, and a quizzical "hmmm" from Sandy before she continues her story.

"Well," she says, "we were surprised. I asked him to tell us more. He went on to say that it's nothing threatening at all, but it is definitely a female spirit. He said, 'I felt her presence constantly in my room.' "

Quite frankly, the Millers probably never dreamed that they would someday be interviewed for a book on ghost stories. They didn't bother at the time to take copious mental notes of what the guest was saying, so the recollections today are a bit sparse. Sandy says she remembers the man saying he did actually see some sort of ghostly form in the room, but doesn't remember if or how he elaborated on it.

"He felt that she was a very happy presence," Sandy says, "and didn't have any idea of why she might be there. But he was positive that the ghost was up there."

The Millers almost dismissed the incident out of hand. One man's idle observations did not a ghost story make. But, there is more.

"I guess it was about two years later," Sandy says, "Nobody had mentioned anything to anybody about the man's statements, but this time it was a woman who mentioned basically the same thing. She had stayed in the same room and she said that she sensed some kind of a presence. She said there was a sensation that there was something in the room with her, and again, she referred to it as a female, a content, unthreatening female spirit. She said it was as if she were back looking for something."

After that second, casual comment on the ghostly goings-on upstairs in the Windward House, the Millers started to take the claims more seriously.

"We had another guest after her, another woman," Sandy continues, "who mentioned the same basic experience again. She, too, felt the presence of a female spirit in that same room."

The room in question is now actually two rooms and a bath.

The upper floors of the inn are reached either by the ample staircase that leads up from the living room, or by a narrow, twisting "back stairs" that has all the trappings of a staircase one would expect to lead to a "haunted" room.

The Wicker Room is delightfully-appointed, bright and comprises one large chamber with a double bed, another smaller room with a single bed and a private bath equipped with a footed tub and pedestal wash basin.

Does the ghost of a young woman really occupy the Wicker Room? The testimony over the years has seemed to confirm that possibility. Assuming there has been no collusion, assuming that each of the guests who slept in the room were independent of one another, then it is safe to assume that something just might be happening on the third floor of the Windward House.

Scores of people have stayed in the Wicker Room since the Millers' establishment of Windward House. Only a handful have reported any strange sensations, and even fewer have labelled them as supernatural. But the aforementioned reports, coupled with one more, just might be convincing enough to warrant serious thought about the matter of ghosts.

That one more report came from a woman who has stayed at the Windward House on several occasions. She became the first person to actually submit a claim that she saw the spirit of the woman of the Wicker Room.

Sandy Miller's recollection of the episode is simple: "She mentioned to us that she walked into the room once and saw a young woman's ghost sitting on the bed."

It was as simple as that. The guest opened the door to the Wicker Room, looked up and saw the ethereal vision of the young spirit, sitting on the edge of the bed. In the second or so it took to deal with the apparition, it vanished.

The intent of the stories in this book is not to conclude and affirm that ghosts do exist. Anyone who claims to know for certain that spectral remains of the dead walk in our time and through our spaces is a fool.

All we can do is listen to those who say they have encountered unexplainable happenings such as those above and in succeeding pages. Then, we can reason for ourselves. Do ghosts exist? Does the spirit of a young woman linger in the Wicker Room? Only you, the reader can answer those questions, and only to your own satisfaction.

THE GHOST OF HIGBEE BEACH

One of the wildest, most ruggedly beautiful and sometimes controversial beaches of New Jersey is not on the Atlantic Ocean. It is Higbee Beach, on the bay side of Cape May.

Its natural state has been ensured by the fact that it is a land restricted to certain uses, and is a wildlife refuge. Higbee Beach is relatively remote, and a certain effort must be made to reach it. The most interesting time to see it, despite its summertime activity, just might be on a gray and grim winter's morning, or on a brisk and brash day during the summer when the worshippers of the sun are somewhere else.

Then, and only then, will the full impact of Higbee Beach be felt.

The pathway from the end of the road to the beach is a wide gap through the undulating sand dunes that frame the sandy strand itself.

Twisted trees and scattered underbrush give the dunes a foreboding look. It is quite easy to conjure up visions of pirates landing on the quiet beach below and lugging their treasure chests into the cedar hummocks for burial. Maybe it really happened there sometime long ago. Maybe, just maybe, their ghosts still haunt those dunes.

There are several versions of popular, time-worn legends about ghosts at Higbee Beach. They vary from the tale of the ghost of old man Higbee himself, to the presence of a slave who kept a lifelong vigil over Higbee's grave long after his master was buried near the beach.

In the research, questioning and interviewing phase of the compilation of this book, the authors asked dozens of people at random if they knew of any ghost stories connected to Cape May.

Eventually, the word spread in certain circles that two writers were seeking tales of the supernatural, and preferably personal experiences with things that go bump in the night.

The result of one of those interviews is the story of the ghost of Higbee Beach, as told by a middle-aged Cherry Hill, New Jersey, woman who responded to the authors' call for encounters with the unknown.

Let us call her Donna. It is not her real name, but in exchange for permission to use her story, anonymity was guaranteed. The story is so strange, and the woman's homelife, work and reputation is so ordinary, that she felt she'd rather not have her friends and fellow employees know that on at least two occasions on Cape May, she had a brush with a ghost.

Donna was visibly shaken and apprehensive about telling her story, but after two or three cups of coffee in a Fisherman's Wharf restaurant one morning, she opened up.

"Well, first of all, let me point out that I don't consider myself to be psychic, or have any talents that would let me contact the dead, or anything like that," she said. "Really, nothing like what happened to me that day on Higbee Beach ever happened before or since. I really live a sort of dull life.

"I must say that I am a nature nut. Not nature food and all that, but birds and animals and plants. You know, the beauty of it all. That's why I love Cape May so much. It's nice to get down here on weekends, especially since my normal contact with nature is the Cooper River, and that isn't much.

"Anyway, you're going to have to trust me on this. There were no witnesses to what happened up on Higbee Beach that day. I was all alone. Well, all alone except for whatever that was that I heard and saw.

"My husband and I and another couple were down at Cape May for a weekend in November a couple of years ago. It's my favorite time to come down here, although we come down maybe fifteen or twenty weekends a year.

"We were staying as we always did, and still do, at one of the nice old Victorian hotels in town. We got down on Friday night and were staying over until Sunday. Well, on Saturday morning, I got up real early. I mean, it was like 4 o'clock or something. I couldn't get back to sleep, so I figured that I would take a walk. Better yet, I thought, I'd take a ride out to Higbee Beach and wander around.

"It was still dark when I got there. I parked in that little circle at the end of the road and walked into the preserve. I guess I really wasn't supposed to be there at that time, but there was nobody else around.

"I should point out that we didn't do any drinking that night before, and I am totally against things like drugs and whatever, so I was cold sober and straight. Well, I walked maybe halfway to the crest of the dunes when I heard a scratching noise just up ahead. I slowed down and, I guess, sort of hid for a second off to the side. It startled me a little.

"As I kind of cowered over in the underbrush, I kept looking up ahead and, well, I couldn't believe my eyes. Up there, on the spot where the dunes drop onto the beach itself, was a man. Well, it was something like a man.

"I wasn't scared, like, for my safety. When I saw the figure up ahead I somehow knew in an instant that it wasn't a real person who could harm me. I knew somehow, right away, that it was, well, it was a ghost!"

Donna paused a second to compose herself. A young-looking woman in her early 40s, Donna fidgeted with her curly brown hair as she continued her story.

"There really isn't much to it, now that I sit here and tell you. All I remember is that there was this old-looking man up ahead, maybe twenty feet, just standing at the crest of a little rise, looking right toward me, but somehow right past me.

"It was as if he didn't know I was there. I stared right at the figure and could make out certain details. The sun was just coming up, and you could start to see the colors of the day and whatnot, but this man, this figure, was a little unusual. It didn't seem to have any color. It was a pale gray, and almost glowing. It seemed to have the light that you get when you put one of those phosphorescent key-chains or whatever under a bright light and then watch it glow in the dark. It wasn't bright, but it was very notice-able.

"Okay, now here's the really strange part. I started to

walk up through the sand, closer to the figure. Hey, big brave girl here! Actually, after the first shock of seeing this man, or whatever, up there, I didn't feel scared. And normally I'm not the most fearless person in the world. But somehow, and I know it sounds weird, but somehow I felt comfortable with whoever or whatever was up there.

"So, I got a little closer and I noticed a couple of things. His pants were too short, almost tattered at the cuffs. He was wearing kind of a sash instead of a belt, and his tee-shirt was very dirty and tattered.

"Now, this all took maybe ten or twenty seconds. He stood there, motionless that long. Then, I heard something. At first I thought it came from the man, and I thought that maybe this figure was real, and the light of dawn was playing tricks. All I remember hearing was a whispering sound followed by a giggle or something like that. Like I said, it seemed to come from where the man was standing.

"Well, he—this figure—looked like he heard whatever I heard, too. He slowly turned around, and started to walk. Well, as I remember, it was not so much a walk, but more like a coast. It was just like, and I hate to say this because it sounds so silly, but it was just like you'd imagine in some ghost movie. He moved without moving his legs, if you can picture that.

"The figure just glided, up and over the hill, and disappeared. It was really strange. So, I got back into the main part of the path and started up the hill. I don't know what came over me. I guess I should have gone back to the car and gotten the heck out of there, but I felt that I should go up to where he was and see whatever I could see.

"I reached the point where he was standing, and there was nothing out of the ordinary. I do remember that there were no footprints in the sand, but I guess that didn't mean much. The sand was all lumpy and bumpy anyway, and specific footprints would be hard to determine.

"I looked down onto the beach, and I almost fainted. There, halfway between me and the water, was the man, well, the ghost. It was coasting or gliding smoothly over the sand toward the water. And, in the distance, I could hear that whispering or giggling sound. It really did sound like a human voice, maybe right at the water's edge. There were no waves to speak of that morning, and I think I could tell the difference between some sound of animals or birds or whatever, and what it was that I was hearing.

"I followed that figure as it slowly went toward the water, and I wondered what would happen next. Well, it didn't take long. The figure went up, closer and closer to the water, and eventually just went right in the water. It just kept on gliding until it was knee-deep, then shoulder-deep, and then all the way in the water. That was the last I saw of it. That's all."

Donna took another swig of a third cup of coffee as she arched her eyebrows, shrugged and punctuated her strange story with one more, "that's all."

She said she stood at the top of the dune for several minutes, wondering if what she had seen was real or imagined. She knew all along, though, that it was absolutely real, and absolutely frightening.

She continued her story. "The sound seemed to get a little louder and clearer as the ghost entered the water and disappeared. When he disappeared, though, the sound stopped. It was then that I realized that what I just witnessed was very strange and, I figured, very frightening.

"I lingered a while on the beach, waiting for whatever might happen next, but after about a half an hour or so, nothing did, so I left and went back to the hotel.

"I had left a note for my husband that I was going to Higbee Beach and I'd probably be back before 8 a.m. Under the circumstances, I got back about 6:30. My husband was just getting up for a shower when I got back into the room. He asked how my morning on the beach went. I thought for a split-second and said, 'well, honey, nothing unusual.'

"Quite honestly, I was more scared to tell my husband what happened than I was when I saw the ghost. I knew he'd think I was completely nuts, and make a joke out of the whole thing.

"To tell the truth, I still never told him anything about it. Maybe after this is in your book I'll have him read it and then tell him that I was the weirdo who saw the ghost on Higbee Beach that morning.

"I know he'll laugh about it, and maybe you are too. But I swear to you that everything I told you was true. Whether it was really a ghost or not, well, who could ever tell? But it was very, very strange and I'll never forget it."

WINTERWOOD, AND OTHER HAUNTED HOUSES

There are numerous "haunted houses" scattered through Cape May County. In addition to the Windward House's story in another chapter of this book, at least two other Victorian inns in Cape May are reportedly visited by ghosts. There are also old stories of ghostly sightings along the cape's many beaches.

It is alleged that spectral figures have been seen on Congress Street in Cape May, near the site of the former Windsor Hotel. Another hotel in town is supposedly where a strange, faceless figure roams a second floor balcony in search of its head.

A salty fisherman from North Cape May told the authors that he has been "spooked" by a ghostly figure that has been seen by more than one man at Schellinger's Landing.

Spirits have been reported roaming around the beach near Cape May Point lighthouse, and some say the John Holmes House, which is home of the Cape May County Historical Museum, is also home to a mysterious, ghostly figure that has been both seen and heard in its ancient rooms and corridors.

But the best-known of all Cape May haunted houses is the Hildreth House near Rio Grande.

The original house, built in the early 1700s and actually moved to its present site in the late 1800s, has been altered and rebuilt many times. It is, today, a stately place, winged with additions that serve as "Winterwood," one of the finest Christmas gift shops in the United States.

Briefly, the Hildreth family was one of the founding clans of Cape May. Their family history co-mingles at times with that of another key family, the Hands.

The house itself, and more properly the land upon which it was built, can be traced as far back as the early 1600s, and is thus one of the oldest continually inhabited parcels in Cape May County.

There are several legends connected to the old Hildreth House. One involves the story of a British soldier who defected from his army during the Revolution and was given safe haven in the Hildreth House. In return for his asylum, the soldier, who was a skilled carver, supposedly crafted the intricate mantelpiece in the central room of the first floor. That very same mantel can be seen (usually behind hundreds of ornaments and strands of tinsel and garland) in the middle room of the Christmas shop.

The ghost of Winterwood, however, is generally referred to as a "she," and specifically as "Hester."

Hester Hildreth was one of the last residents of the house who still carried the family name. She died in 1948 and her fellow spinster sister, Lucille, died six years later. The property was maintained by a distant relative for a while, but eventually fell out of the hands of the Hildreths.

Today, many people have reported odd occurrences within the walls of the house. Both the present and former owners of the house, as well as employees of the gift shop and contractors doing work there have had experiences there.

Those experiences include hearing voices long after all customers had gone, and when the one, two or three people inside were certain they were alone.

Those voices were almost always those of women, two women conversing in distinct, but somehow indeterminable words. Some have attributed the voices to those of the last of the Hildreths, Lucille and Hester.

Hester has also been blamed for the eerie footsteps that have been heard ascending a back staircase from time to time, and for the various thumps and rumblings that have been heard in the rooms of the house.

Workmen have had tools scattered about by unseen forces, and employees have watched incredulously as wall-mounted displays have slid from their hooks. Quick checks revealed that it would have been next to impossible for the displays to fall from the wall without some kind of assistance.

There have been actual sightings of ghostly figures at the Hildreth House. One person reported the apparition of a white-robed, mysterious person who glided across the lawn from the house to the area of the old family burial ground, and simply vanished into thin air.

Another person claimed that a cloaked figure, misty and shadowy, crossed in front of her at a doorway in the house.

Some folks treat the odd goings-on at Winterwood with a playful benevolence. Hence, "Hester" has been adopted as a "resident spook." Others, however, have been genuinely frightened by whatever or whoever lurks within the walls of the old house, and are not as frivolous about the matter.

ELIZABETH, THE GHOST OF THE WASHINGTON INN

They call the ghost Elizabeth.

Nobody really knows why, it was just something the staff members at the Washington Inn chose, for no apparent reason.

Perhaps there never was an Elizabeth who lived at the old inn. Perhaps nothing untoward ever happened to anyone who ever lived at the big building at Washington and Jefferson Streets in Cape May.

Perhaps, just perhaps, there isn't even a ghost at the Washington Inn.

But try telling that to those who take the presence of Elizabeth very seriously.

The proud history of the Washington Inn includes a list of owners and operators that reads like a Who's Who of Cape May County history.

The plot upon which the inn is located was purchased by Lemuel Leaming in 1843—a princely sum of seventy-five dollars for forty-two acres.

The first structure on the land was erected by Lemuel Swain, Jr., who eventually turned it over to Aaron Cromwell, Jr. The home, it is said, resembled George Washington's beloved Mount Vernon.

That original home went through many architectural and aesthetic changes over the years. Its tall front pillars were removed by subsequent owners, and one resident even placed the home on rollers and moved it within the confines of the corner lot. After moving it to satiate his desire for a more pleasant position, farther from the street, one Thomas Quigg changed his mind and put it back on rollers for another move, back to its original location.

The building's service as an inn did not begin until 1940, when Martha Hand and her daughter opened their home to wayfarers.

The operation of the inn continued through several proprietors until 1979 when its present owners, Toby and Rona Craig, purchased the business.

The Craigs have added a Victorian cocktail lounge, a charming greenhouse, and have made many more improvements on the inside and outside of the handsome building.

If some theories on the source of ghostly activity can be believed, there is much within the walls of the Washington Inn upon which to hang a ghost hunter's hat.

The main bar of the inn was hand-crafted by Toby Craig from chestnut doors salvaged from a Cape May home.

The leaded glass-highlighted bar back is a German wardrobe, brought to America by Toby's grandmother in the early twentieth century.

The many alternations, additions, renovations and permanent furniture placements could all contribute to the possibility of supernatural activity in the inn.

Indeed, some researchers into the paranormal believe that pieces of furniture can hold within them energy that could be released, or read, from time to time.

If that theory is to be believed to any degree, then the Washington Inn is a prime candidate for ghostly goings-on.

Most of what has happened at the Washington Inn has taken place around the central entrance to the inn.

That entranceway was once graced by a staircase that led to the second floor. The Craigs had the stairway removed to accommodate their patrons and facilitate the operation of the restaurant. The cashier's station was relocated, and a partition was placed on the right.

It is usually a gentle woman's voice that can be heard in this foyer. The Craigs, and those staff members who claim to have heard the voice, do not deny the strange occurrences, although Toby does remain somewhat the skeptic.

Even more of a skeptic was Toby's father, who spent much time working at the inn. One time, he was working in an upstairs office, just at the top of the staircase.

He distinctly heard a soft, female voice calling "dad . . .dad," in what he described as a very identifiable Eastern Shore accent.

He immediately recognized the voice as that of his daughter-in-law, Rona, who did, in fact, call him "dad." He didn't give much thought to it until he realized that Rona was not in the inn that day.

After his brief but disconcerting encounter, Mr. Craig vowed to never again work in the inn alone. And, there is one less skeptic when the topic of Elizabeth, the ghost of the Washington Inn, is brought up.

Rona Craig jests that Elizabeth probably picked up her distinctive Eastern Shore accent from the many times Rona has called for "Dad" Craig over the years.

Mrs. Craig says there is no immediate fear when Elizabeth calls your name. The first reaction is that another flesh-and-blood person is speaking. Only after fruitless searching is it revealed that there is no one nearby, and then the goosebumps begin to rise.

It is estimated that the majority of waitresses and hostesses who have toiled at the Washington Inn over the years have heard their names called out by the ghostly girl they call Elizabeth.

Most of the times, the incidents took place when the women were setting up their stations in the evening or before the restaurant actually opened.

Softly, the voice would whisper "Laura. . ." or "Dianne. . ." or "Onja. . ."

Onja, a long-time employee at the inn, has been particularly vexed by Elizabeth. Michael Craig, who with his brother, David, represent a third generation of Craigs involved with the inn, tells a tale of Onja's most unusual and unexplained experience with Elizabeth.

She was working in the interior part of the restaurant when she plainly heard her name being called from the porch. "Onja," the ghostly voice uttered. Obligingly, Onja walked to the porch to see who was calling her.

"Onja," the voice called again. And again Onja cautiously ventured out to the porch. She assumed it was another waitress, Mary Lou, calling her. The voice repeated her name two or three more times, and Onja was beginning to tire of the whole matter.

She had enough, and in a huff stormed out to the porch one more time. She sternly reprimanded Mary Lou for her practical jokery. A stunned Mary Lou looked at Onja with innocence in her eyes. She swore she never once called Onja's name, and she was the only person on the porch at the time!

Onja had also had her pen misplaced, only to be found later in a spot she knew she could not have placed it.

One waitress reported the Elizabeth, or whatever the true identity of whatever energy is in the Washington Inn, once tossed a glass for attention.

A previous owner of the inn has agreed that there is a presence in the building, but declined to elaborate.

Rona Craig has had her own name called out by the unseen woman. Still, she has no fear.

Actually, Rona would like to know more about who or what haunts her inn. There have never been any real unpleasantries, and no patron has reported anything unusual.

Much of the unexplained activity has ceased since the central staircase was removed. Still, there is a certain sensation in the lovely old inn that maybe Elizabeth is still there, sadly calling out the names of anyone who might listen to whatever story she might have to tell.

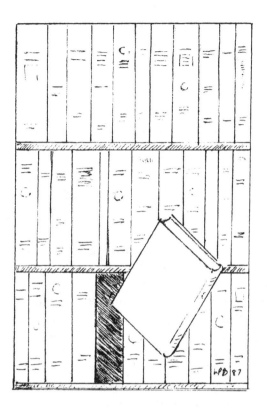

THE HAUNTED BOOK STORE

Perhaps you have purchased this volume at Keltie's News and Books in the Washington Street Mall in the lovely commercial hub of Cape May.

Thank you for choosing our book. And, the next time you browse around Keltie's, listen closely. Is that laughter you hear coming from a corner? Have a look. Is there someone really in that corner?

Look around again. Was that a wispy figure you saw

over against one of the walls? Did it seem to materialize and vanish before your eyes?

Could it then be that this busy and popular shop is haunted? You bet it is!

Or, so say at least two of the couples who have owned and operated Keltie's over the last several years.

Who or what haunts the old shop? There are a couple of theories, and either is plausible.

Before we venture forth into the actual ghost stories, let us note that the building in which Keltie's prosperous business is carried out dates back well over a century. In fact, the structure was once somewhere else. Recent architectural surveys and contractors' inspections confirmed that the building could be up to 140 years old, and may have been moved to its present location from a beach front site.

In the not-too-distant past, the building served many functions. The Knerr sisters operated a millinery shop inside a portion of it years ago, and it also housed an attorney's office up front and a dentist's office in the rear.

The Knerr sisters and the dentist, a Dr. Loomis, figure in the thinking of Gene and Josie Davids, the present owners of the book shop, and Jim and Terri Keltie, namesakes and previous owners of the business.

The Kelties have both had brushes with a mysterious, ghostly figure in the store.

It all started when Terri Keltie claimed that a pallid, barely discernible image materialized in the shop, passed by her and continued on its way until it seemingly vanished.

The phenomenon repeated itself many times. The figure, said Mrs. Keltie, was dressed in a white coat similar to that a dentist would wear, and seemed to be translucent.

Terri cautiously told her husband about her experiences, and as she might have expected, he rejected her story and dismissed it as a product of an overactive imagination.

Eventually Jim Keltie changed his mind. There was a very good reason.

One quiet night, Jim was sitting in the upstairs living room when he was distracted by something a few feet away. He looked up to see the clear image of a man in a white coat standing in the middle of the room. The spectre faded almost as quickly as it appeared, but Jim Keltie's opinion of his wife's encounters had changed forever.

Terri Keltie noted that the shadowy form made no sound. She said as it passed her it seemed to be looking directly at her, but showed no emotion. "He came out of the kitchen," she said, "and walked toward the front of the building. You could go right past him. You would think it was somebody coming at you. When he passed, you felt a very soft breeze."

She and her husband lived with the spirit in their home and shop for several years. One day, Mrs. Keltie happened to mention her experiences to a friend. The friend told her that she could rid the building of the ghost with a simple exorcism. She told her to simply encounter the spirit and repeat, "Doctor Loomis, you don't belong here. Now go in peace."

This, of course, is a legitimate approach to the expulsion of spirits in any home. Usually performed by a medium or psychic, the exhortation has been known to rid houses of their haunts.

Sure enough, Mrs. Keltie tried it, and it seemed to work. One night, the ghostly figure appeared in a hallway, and began its nocturnal sojourn. "Go in peace, Dr. Loomis," Terri Keltie said, and the ghost disappeared, never to be seen again.

But the departure of Dr. Loomis' ghost may have opened the doors of the great beyond for the entrance of other spirits that may inhabit the book store.

Gene and Josie Davids, who now operate the book shop, have had their own incidents with spooky happenings within the walls of the building.

The Davids often keep long hours at the store, and it has almost always been after the store had closed that the strange events took place.

There is a possibility that the weakened energy or "ghost" of Dr. Loomis still dwells in the building. Josie Davids said that while she and her husband were living over the store, a dark phantom once appeared in the bedroom. She said it appeared and disappeared swiftly, and there was no time to make out any physical details.

More profound were the other episodes of the unexplained, which took two basic forms.

Imagine, if you will (with apologies to the late Rod Serling), that you are alone in the book store, late at night. You cock an ear toward the front of the store and you hear the muffled sound of conversation, and then giggling.

You know that there is no one else in the place, and there is no activity on Washington Street at that time. Still, you listen intently. The giggling is that of females. The conversation is indistinguishable. But it is out there, somewhere, and most definitely is inside the building.

Such is the experience of Josie Davids. She has heard the giggling sounds, as has her husband. Gene Davids has also seen the shadowy form seemingly walking aimlessly from one room to another.

Almost whimsically, the Davids have associated the laughter to the Knerr sisters. They do not dismiss the shadowy presence as being that of Dr. Loomis.

While the apparition and the disembodied laughter can be vexing, yet another periodic occurrence can be downright frightening.

Both Josie and Gene have witnessed it. Together or alone, both have watched as books mysteriously fell from securely-stacked shelves.

They gazed incredulously as one book seemed to work its way out of a stack and dropped. Then another, and another, fluttering to the floor as if forcefully pried out by ghostly hands.

Over the many occasions that the book-moving took place, the Davids have tried in vain to explain it all.

Gravity? Hardly. The books were most definitely moved by an energy that was much more powerful that even gravity. They traveled first out of the shelves and then dropped.

The wind? In no way. There is simply no wind, no breeze and no gust of air of any kind capable of pushing the books out of the shelves so selectively and so powerfully.

A practical joker? No, the Davids were alone in the building.

There really was no logical explanation.

At wit's end, and more angry than scared, Josie once uttered, in a kind of knee-jerk reaction to one of the book droppings, "Look, if you are going to make this mess, then you clean it up!"

Oddly enough, since that strong warning, not another book has wedged its way out of the shelves and onto the floor.

But have the ghosts of Keltie's News and Books been evicted?

Gene and Josie cannot be certain. The store still becomes an eerie, quiet place when all the shoppers have gone. The strong memories of the books dropping, the muffled laughter, and even the time the blender in the kitchen turned itself on will linger forever.

"Nobody believes us," Josie laments. "They think we're gone," she chuckles. Josie further believes that whatever has happened there, and whatever has caused it is not malevolent by nature.

It would stand to reason that the ghosts, should they be those of the Knerr sisters or the dentist, would be gentle and well-meaning.

"I'm a very spookable person," Josie says. "I'd be out

the door in a flash if I thought something mean would happen."

In all likelihood, there are still spirits inside Keltie's. Stop by sometime. Browse through the stacks of books and magazines. But beware, if you feel that unnerving sensation that someone is looking over your shoulder, don't turn around!

HE'S STILL HERE

"Every night, like clockwork, he'd be here," said the attractive redhead who for more than a dozen years was the favorite waitress of the old man with the one dark eyeglass lens and the peculiar aroma of baby powder.

"It was as if we were his only friends and maybe I was his best friend," she continued.

The setting is a Cape May beach front restaurant whose present owners prefer the authors not pinpoint. "I know it sounds quite foolish, maybe," one of the partners in the restaurant said, "but I'd just as soon let the incident pass, if it ever really will."

That incident is the recurring visitation of the ghost of the old man who still frequents the restaurant.

The proprietors, who wish to remain nameless, authorized their waitress to tell the tale. "Peggy (not her real name, either, at her request) knows all the details. I am familiar with the old man, and how often he came here, and how his ghost supposedly still comes here."

Supposedly?

Don't use that word around Peggy, or any of a dozen or so witnesses to the spectral appearances of the old man.

In fact, each of the restaurant's owners will vouch for Peggy. They have seen the old man, too. Years after he passed away.

Peggy set the stage for the ghost story with a background on the old man.

"Some people said he was one of those men who had been very rich, lost his fortune, and became the next thing to a street person," Peggy said.

"I had heard that he was in the food business up in Philly, and operated some big business in the distribution center down under the Walt Whitman Bridge. Supposedly, he had some personal problems, something like his wife being very ill and mounting large medical bills. Well, they say he lost it all and moved into some small home he owned down here in Cape May.

"Anyway, he started coming into the restaurant about a month or so after I started working here," she continued. "Right from day one, he struck me as a little odd. There were just these little things about him. He wore a battered old hat, and, now this may sound silly, but he smelled like baby powder. It was a pleasant smell, but something I'd never expect from an old guy like him.

"There were a couple of other weird things. He had a huge ring on one of his fingers. I don't know what kind of stone it was, but it was big and looked like a gem. He always sat in the corner booth over there, and the light always caught the ring, bouncing reflections off the ceiling and walls.

"The most I remember about his face was his eyeglasses. It was very strange that one lens, the left one I think, was darker than the other. It was a little distracting at first, but I got used to it. I just couldn't see how he was comfortable with one so much darker, but I guess he was.

"Well, that's basically all I remember. He dressed fairly normal for a man of his age, about 65 or so, and was very courteous, quiet and well-mannered.

"It was June of 1980 when he started coming in, and you know, right from the beginning, we struck up a kind of friendship.

"He used to pick up the morning paper sometimes, most of the time, and take it to that corner table with him.

He'd always return it to the end of the counter when he left. He would chat with all of us, gripe about the weather or the economy or something, and maybe tell a joke.

"Oh, yes, his name was Don. What was very strange, and kind of cute, is that he would sign the check almost every day. You know, I would write on it, 'Thank You, Peg,' and he would use his pen and write underneath it, 'You're Welcome, Don!' I thought that was funny, and we'd always chuckle about it."

Peggy giggled with fond remembrance as she recounted the days Don would stop by the old Victorian restaurant. She continued her story and the smile faded from her lips.

"Don came in almost every day at the same time, just about four o'clock. I never bothered to ask what he did during the day. Maybe he worked, maybe not. It wasn't important. Well, one afternoon, four o'clock came and went, and no Don. He was so much of a routine part of my day that at about two minutes after four I noticed he wasn't around and wondered about it. By about 4:30, my wonder turned to worry.

"All of us were a little concerned. We really missed the old guy."

It was about an hour later, about 5:30 in the evening, when something happened that at the time was no cause for alarm, just curiosity.

"There were only a handful of people in the restaurant at the time," Peg recalled, "and I was behind the counter with another girl. Everything was fairly quiet.

"The next thing we knew, there was a very distinct odor of baby powder coming from the corner. It was the corner where Don always sat.

"The other waitress noticed it the same time I did. She looked at me and said she smelled it and laughed about it. She said it was 'leftover Don,' or something like that. We both felt that it could very well have been just a whiff that really was left over from the last time Don was there. Anyway, we didn't give it too much thought.

"But then, we were startled as the newspaper, which was in the middle of the counter top, just whooshed off the counter like a strong wind blew it away. The only thing was, there was no strong wind. We both saw it blow off the counter, and we both would swear that there was not any wind or breeze or anything that could have moved it like that.

"We both faked smiles and kidded around that it must have been a ghost. Little did we know what was to follow!"

What was to follow would be enough to boggle the mind of the most sane and sober of humans.

"Not much of anything happened any more that night," Peggy said. "But the next day, everybody in the restaurant had the shock of their lives.

"Just after I got to work, sometime before noon, one of the other regulars came in, sat down, and started to shoot the breeze. Very matter-of-factly, he said that the old guy, Don, that always came in later in the afternoon, was found dead in his room down the street last night.

"I asked, very cautiously, if he knew what time they found the body. He said, 'oh, I believe it was sometime late last night, but they say he died around five or five-thirty.'

"Right away, I started to think about it. Almost instinctively I put two and two together. Now, I'm not a ghost nut or anything, but I have read quite a bit on omens and intuition and ghosts, and I thought right away about what had happened on the counter and in the corner of the restaurant the previous night, just about the time old Don probably died. I got goosebumps."

Peggy said the other waitress who had watched the newspaper fly off the counter and who had taken a whiff of the baby powder aroma wasn't working the day the customer made the revelation about Don's death, so she called her to tell the story.

"She knew full well what we had experienced that eve-

44

ning," Peggy said, "but mocked me when I put any significance to any of it. It was almost a friendship-threatening attitude. I'm not superstitious, and I did not claim for certain that what happened had any ghostly meaning, but it certainly was a coincidence, if nothing else.

"The rest gets kind of strange, and to tell the truth, I am not sure I really believe it all. I mean, if I heard someone else telling the story, I guess I would think that they were a little nuts!"

Nonetheless, Peggy continued. She masked her own emotions of fear, awe and confusion with occasional smirks and shrugs. Still, it was quite obvious that the experience she related had a most profound and unsettling influence on her.

"I guess the first thing was the old guy's funeral," she said. "I was working, it was getting busier, and although I tried half-heartedly, I couldn't keep track of Don's obituary or death notice. I wasn't sure when the funeral was to be and I guess I missed it whenever it might have been in the paper."

But perhaps Peggy was reminded of the funeral in a bizarre fashion.

"A couple of days after I learned Don was dead," I had just come to work again when I was cleaning some tables from the breakfast crowd. One of them was the corner table Don always sat in when he came here.

"You can believe this or not, but sure enough, there was the aroma of baby powder again. Well, again I reasoned that it was just left over from his old visits, or maybe someone else who sat there earlier used baby powder, or maybe it was my imagination. I tried every excuse I could think of, but nothing really worked. Deep down inside, I felt that Don's spirit was still there, and this was his way of letting me know.

"Then, I thought that maybe I was going crazy, thinking such things. But I gave it some really deep thought and I knew that it might be possible."

Peggy gazed to the ceiling as she tried to compose herself. The memories of the episodes that followed were not particularly pleasant.

"A few days passed by. I think there was a weekend in between, and maybe I had a couple of days off somewhere along the line. Anyway, it was a few days until anything else happened, she said.

"Another girl and I were in our usual positions in the afternoon, over by the kitchen door at the end of the counter. There were a few customers at the tables, and the usual couple of hangers-on at the counter. Well, all of us—and I mean everyone in the place—sort of jumped when all of a sudden the newspaper on the counter just kind of fluttered up about six or eight inches off the counter and flew in many separated pages onto the floor.

"It was again as if a strong wind had taken it. But we all knew there was no wind at all. The other waitress said it must have been the air current created when the kitchen door swings open and closed. Just for her sake, I agreed, although I knew better. In fact, I stayed on a little later that night until after she left, and put the paper back on the counter where it was. Then, I went to the kitchen door and swung it open and shut many times. The paper wouldn't budge. Of course, I knew it wouldn't.

When asked why she felt she knew it wasn't a breeze or the current from the door, she had a firm answer: "Because for the first time, I started to believe in ghosts. Don's ghost."

Peggy continued, "I almost wanted that old man's ghost to be there. I knew that if it would, it wouldn't do any harm to anyone.

"Well, the next sign I got that old Don may be hanging around was another whiff of baby powder, right over at his old table. Once in a while, out of the corner of my eye, I even thought I saw something in that corner, but I wouldn't put much stock in it. I figured my imagination was starting to go a little wild."

But after a while, Peggy said she knew that whatever was tormenting her was more than her imagination.

"The really strange stuff started late in the summer of 1980," she said. "One morning, this middle-aged couple came into the restaurant. My eyes caught them as soon as they came in, and I watched as the woman took a deep breath and looked around. She motioned to her husband that they should go over to their left, over to the corner where Don always sat.

"The woman was nice looking, somewhere near fifty years old, I guess, and was very well dressed. So was the man. Anyway, they asked me if they could sit at the corner table. I nodded to them that they could.

"Right away, as I was handing them their menus, the woman started to look around. She slowly turned her head and gazed away into space. It was as if something in the restaurant had gotten her attention.

"I had no idea what was going on, but then again you see a lot of strange people and things in a place like this over a summer. The woman put her menu down, ordered coffee and the breakfast special, and then called me back to the table as I was walking back to place the order.

"She looked at me very seriously, and then asked a question that I thought would make me pass out. She asked if anyone ever told her there were spirits in the restaurant.

"Now, I thought, what a strange question. She even asked it as if she knew it was a little strange. Still, she told me she was serious, and that she had a gift for telling such things.

"She wasn't mysterious, you know, like some kind of weirdo in a cape, but she calmly said there was some sort of field of energy in the restaurant, and it was at its strongest right where she was sitting. Need I tell you that she was sitting where Don used to sit?"

Peggy said she swallowed hard and told the woman that she would talk to her more after she placed their order.

"I didn't know what to make of it at first," she said.

"One of my first thoughts is that it might be a set-up, that maybe the other waitress who kidded with me about Don's ghost might have put this woman up to it. Then I thought again, and reasoned that it couldn't be. In fact, later I asked the other girl about it, very slyly, and she scolded me for even thinking about such an idea.

"The couple's order came up, and I took it to them. As they started to eat, the woman nonchalantly said that there was definitely energy in the place, and asked if anything unfortunate had ever happened there. I sort of faked it for a while and told her no. After all, as far as I knew, nothing had. But I was curious. I asked if she could tell me more about whatever it was that she detected. She told me she wasn't sure about a lot of things, but that she could 'read' the place if I wanted to.

"Then I thought that she might have been some fortune teller or something, and the whole deal might wind up costing me money. I think she could detect that in my reaction, and right away she told me that she would like to find out more just for her own sake, and that she would never even think of charging for such a reading.

Then, I thought, the owners would probably never stand for it. Both guys had seen the paper fly off the counter at least a couple of times, and I'm not sure if they ever smelled the baby powder. I was afraid to even ask if this woman could come in sometime, after hours, and 'read' their restaurant. Actually, I guess I would feel silly asking them.

"I told the woman that I would ask the owners, and maybe she could come back and tell me more. I admitted to her that I had my own suspicions about the restaurant, and that table in particular. She told me that she and her husband were staying for a couple of weeks at a nearby B & B, and that I could contact her there.

"Well, I knew I had a challenge. I would have to build up enough nerve to ask the guys if they'd allow such a

thing. About an hour after the couple left, both of the owners were sitting at their usual table, and I went on a break. I
got up the nerve and figured I had nothing to lose. I was
nervous, but I told them my story, and of my meeting with
the woman, and her desire to read the place. They listened,
didn't even bat an eyelash, and said that it would be fine
with them, as long as nobody else knew anything about it
and that they could be present when the woman came back.
Well, I was relieved and happy.

"I called the woman at the place she was staying that
night. She said she had plans for the next day, but could
stop by the day after, preferably in the evening.

"That night, we closed down at about 7:30 and I had
arranged for her to be there at about eight. Sure enough,
she and her husband showed up, and I was there with my
bosses. I felt strange, as if some chintzy scene from a
movie was about to be filmed, and I was to be the main
character.

"They looked quite normal again. He was wearing the
kind of shirt most guys his age down here wear in the
summer, and she was wearing a pretty dress. At first I
thought that it wasn't the way a medium was supposed to
look as she conducted a seance, or whatever.

"We sat down at a table on the other side of the room
from the one Don used to use. She specifically said we
shouldn't sit at that one.

"She didn't waste any time. The five of us sat there
and she started to stare at the wall. I was expecting, well, I
was a little nervous and didn't really know what to expect.

"Soon enough, she looked up toward the ceiling and
started to talk. She said she felt the very strong presence of
a male, probably middle-aged to elderly, and probably the
kind of man who was once involved in the food business.

"I don't mind saying that I almost shit when she said
that. After all, I had heard that old Don once worked at the
Food Distribution Center up in Philly.

"Then, things really got strange. She blinked her eyes and looked very abruptly at me. She asked if a newspaper had ever, in her words, 'acted oddly' in the restaurant.

"I guess you know what that did to me. I gulped, and remembered all the times the newspaper rustled off the counter. I said yes, and she nodded.

"She said that the table over in the corner, the one she and her husband first sat in and the one Don used to use, was the focus of a spiral of energy. She explained that it was the leftover energy of a human life, or something like that, and it could be interpreted as a spirit or ghost.

"Actually, I was quite calm at that point, because she was then affirming everything I believed that was happening."

Peggy added that the woman could have no knowledge of the newspaper incidents, nor of what she deduced from a further "reading."

Peggy said she was amazed. "The woman looked upward again and just kept talking for about two minutes. She said the letter 'D' meant something, that maybe it was the man's name. Then she said, 'Dan, or Don.' And then she said 'tomatoes,' and then some colors and women's names. I really forgot some of the things she rambled on about, but of course when she said 'Don,' it was time for shit number two! And, who knows, maybe Don was a tomato dealer at the Food Distribution Center.

"Well, that was about it. We all took deep breaths and the woman concluded by saying that the restaurant is, as people say, haunted, but that the spirit that haunts it is very kind and eager to please. She said that the only harm it would do is maybe stir something up (like the newspaper) or make itself known somehow else (like the aroma of baby powder)."

Peggy said her bosses watched the entire proceeding with rapt attention, and just shook their heads when it was over. She never said much more to them about it afterward.

"You know, sometimes I really do think I can see Don sitting over in his corner," Peggy said. "I know for sure that I don't, but his memory is so strong. And, of course, I often smell the baby powder, and the newspaper often slides off the counter. Even random customers say they have noticed the smell and many people have seen the paper act up. I have never told any customer about the ghost. Really, I feel that it's none of their concern. If Don's spirit is here, I don't mind at all. He was a kind man, and it's nice to know he had a home in the hereafter."

The authors of this book tried to contact the medium who conducted the interview at the Cape May beach front restaurant that evening. After following several leads, the search finally ended in suburban Baltimore, with a telephone call to her home.

A man answered and confirmed that he was the husband of the woman who "read" the restaurant in Cape May. He said his wife was very interested in the "other side" and did much research on the spirit world. Yes, he said, he remembered the Cape May incident. But no, he would not want to talk about it "on the record" for a book.

He apologized and said he had nothing against our efforts, or against the notion of the recording of ghost stories. His voice seemed to disintegrate rapidly as he offered his reason for declining an interview and hedging on calling his wife to the telephone.

Earlier that day, he told us, he had found his wife dead in their home.

It was our turn to apologize.

THE HAUNTING OF THE HEIRLOOM

An imposing structure, the Heirloom Bed and Breakfast and its associated shops at 601 Columbia Avenue in the thick of Cape May's Historic District.

Imposing, handsome . . .and haunted.

Oh, if the walls of this fine old building could talk!

Built during America's centennial year, the Heirloom did not always enjoy the impeccable reputation its present owners have achieved.

Much in the way of ungainly activity has taken place inside what is now a fine nine-room B & B. Some of its bawdy past remains in the form of furnishings. More of it may remain in the form of the unexplained, unseen and unnerving.

Anthony and Frances Ruggiero, the owners of the Heirloom, will readily admit that the place was once a private gambling club, a speakeasy, and a rather elegant brothel.

Long before the massive, glitzy and glittery casinos of Atlantic City vaulted that town into gambling prominence, the old building of Columbia was bustling with rolling dice, spinning roulette wheels and shuffling cards.

They say that the tidy gambling room was where the second floor parlor now welcomes guests. They say that the bedrooms grouped around it were used to, uh, "entertain" male gamblers who sought even more stimulating activities.

They even say that there was a somewhat clever signalling system that warned the speakeasy proprietors that the local lawmen were on the block.

On the second floor verandah, where visitors now may enjoy leisurely breakfasts, there once was a black woman stationed as a lookout over the streets below.

When the gambling and carousing was in full swing, the woman sat motionlessly on the porch, ostensibly knitting or sewing or occupying herself quietly in some other fashion.

But, when she noticed a police wagon or car or patrolman within close proximity, she would begin to rock steadily and deliberately. The creaky floorboards under the rockers would be the alarm for all inside that trouble was a-brewin', and all illegal activities should be put under wraps, and quickly!

It's that kind of heritage—as if straight from a Hollywood production—that gives the Heirloom its particular character.

There are some peculiar architectural appurtenances to the old building, too. There is a secret doorway from one of the businesses on street level to the Heirloom building. Another doorway served as the nondescript entrance to the bordello and gambling chamber. Customers would enter through what appeared to be a legitimate business (a pharmacy at the time) and be shuffled through the other doors to "the action."

There is even an old, round table in the Heirloom's present parlor, and Anthony Ruggiero is all but certain that it is one of the original gambling tables.

The Heirloom has an even more recent connection to a shadier side of human events. Ruggiero says that William Bradfield, the former Pennsylvania high school principal convicted of murder in the infamous Susan Reinert case of the mid-1980s, stayed at the Heirloom often and attempted to use one of his visits there as an alibi. He said he couldn't have committed the murders of Reinert and her two children in Pennsylvania because he was in Cape May at the time. Mr. Ruggiero said that when Bradfield was there, he made his presence very well known to all others by making noise and drawing attention to himself. Despite his alibi attempts and his boisterous conduct, the judge and jury concluded that he could very well have committed the crimes even if he had stayed at the Heirloom.

Oh, if those walls could talk!

Anthony and Frances Ruggiero are not totally convinced that the Heirloom is haunted. However, they do not hesitate to detail the many unusual events that have taken place there. What's more, others have experienced odd occurrences in the old place.

Frances, a school teacher, and Anthony, an attorney, have had their own share of strange happenings. Once, after securing the inn for the week and heading for their jobs in New York on a Sunday night, they returned the following weekend to a disheartening sight.

They looked in on what they call the "Plum Room" on the third floor and saw that all of the lighter decorations, knick-knacks and dried flower arrangements were strewn helter-skelter around the room. At first, they had the sinking feeling that someone had broken into the inn.

They closely inspected all windows and doors, and discovered that none had been opened. Everything was as secure as the night they left.

There was no sign at all of any forced entry. Puzzled and perhaps a bit frightened, they proceeded to hang things back on the walls from which they fell and place things back on tables from which they were swept.

It is the Plum Room that has drawn most of the Ruggiero's concern. The third floor room has often been the site of unexplained movement and displacement.

One time, the toilet of the Plum Room simply exploded. There was water damage to walls and floors below, and no apparent reason for the incident. A plumber figured it had to be the result of some kind of vibration, but reasoned that nothing could be so violent that it could single out a toilet for damage.

A befuddled electrician was once challenged by other perplexing episodes on the third floor. After a patron reported upon checking out that a light bulb had burned out in the Plum Room bathroom, an employee went to check the matter. She reported to Mary Hackler, who was the innkeeper at the Heirloom at the time, that there was no electricity at all on the third floor.

Mary checked the circuit breakers, and all seemed to be well. Still, there was no electricity on the third floor.

She called an electrician, and while she was waiting for him to arrive, she threw all the circuit breakers. Nothing happened. No electricity.

As she walked away from the breaker box, she heard the sound of the vacuum cleaner on the third floor. It was plugged in, and turned on, but would not work for the other employee. It was whirring away now.

Mary figured that she had solved the problem. She headed back to the third floor and noticed quite plainly that the vacuum cleaner had stopped.

She checked it, saw that it was still turned on and still plugged in. She shook her head and walked back downstairs. As she descended, she was stopped in her tracks as the vacuum cleaner started to whirr away once again.

The electrician arrived and checked the circuit breakers and the general wiring. He found nothing wrong. There was no reasonable explanation for the electrical glitch on the third floor, but to be sure, he replaced the circuit breakers.

It would be folly to use electrical and plumbing malfunctions as the basis for a ghost story. But the ghostly aspect becomes much more clear when the testimony of at least one guest and at least one other is added to the tale.

The guest's story is simple, and it is remembered by Mary Hackler.

One morning, she recalls quite vividly, a young woman

came into the dining room for breakfast and stated, very nonchalantly, that she believed there was a spirit in her room last night.

Mary didn't think much of the proclamation. She did feel, though, that the girl wanted to talk more about whatever was on her mind. She didn't appear to be flippant about the statement, and seemed to be very sincere.

Mary asked her what she meant. The guest told her that sometime in the middle of the night, something passed by and bumped her bed. She knew there was no physical being in the room, but most definitely felt the bump. She said she sat up in bed, and as she did, she felt the very strong sensation of an icy breeze pass by her.

Another time, a patron reported that she had smelled the aroma of perfume in her room. She did not recognize the fragrance and was curious as to its origin, since there were no other women on her floor.

Both of these incidents took place on the third floor, in either the Plum Room or the adjacent Palm Room.

For Anthony and Frances Ruggiero, however, the most telling of all the tales about the possibility of spirits in the Heirloom came from someone Mr. Ruggiero would tend to want to trust and believe: His mother.

The elder Mrs. Ruggiero had often been hesitant when it came to spending any amount of time at her son and daughter-in-law's bed and breakfast in Cape May.

The matter worried Anthony a bit. He wondered why his own mother often declined invitations to stay at the inn.

A couple of days after the Ruggieros spoke with the authors of this book about their ghostly inn, they were at their New York home for dinner with Anthony's parents.

The after-dinner conversation turned to a mention by Anthony of his meeting with the authors. He told his parents that the topic was ghosts. He barely got the words out when his mother shot out to her husband, "You see, I told you there was a presence in that building!"

It was then revealed, to the surprise of Anthony and Frances, that the reason mother hesitated to stay at their inn was that she felt uncomfortable there because she felt it was haunted.

Mrs. Ruggiero further stated that she believed the "presence" or "spirit" to be that of a woman, and probably one of the girls who once worked "the world's oldest profession" in the former bordello.

She added that she felt all along that the ghost walked the Heirloom's third floor.

She had discussed her feelings about the place before with Anthony's father, but made him vow to never tell anyone about her concerns.

Likewise, the younger Ruggiero never mentioned to his mother that others had had the same feelings about the third floor and its spectral inhabitant.

In one fell swoop, a long family mystery had been solved. But one mystery remains intact. The mystery, of course, of the ghost of the third floor of the Heirloom Bed and Breakfast in Cape May.

There have been no visions of ghoulish creatures with arms outstretched, clanking their chains down the hallway. No moans have been heard, no shrieks in the night, and no pair of red eyes glowed through a window pane.

Still, the disheveled room, the finicky utilities, the wisp of air, whiff of perfume and the bump in the night all contribute to the sense of heritage and, in a sense, warmth, that is the hallmark of the Heirloom.

A DENNISVILLE GHOST

One of the names that recurs in Cape May history is Ludlam. Its most permanent and noteworthy legacies include Ludlam Beach on the Atlantic and the handsome Henry Ludlam Inn on route 47 just south of Dennisville.

Henry Ludlam settled in South Jersey in the 18th century and established a homestead of his vast land holdings that stretched nearly from bay to sea.

In his life, he married three times, and his wives Hannah, Patience and Mary are all buried near his remains. He fathered nine, and in addition to being a prominent and successful attorney, he is credited with organizing the first public school in New Jersey.

While no one claims that Henry Ludlam's ghost walks the ancient halls of his old home, the owners of what is now a charming five-room bed-and-breakfast on the shore of a picturesque lake will readily admit that there is more than meets the eye in the Ludlam house.

Seemingly picayune things have happened to just about anybody who has lived in the house: Doors opened and closed on their own, lights went off and on for no apparent reason and phantom knocks were heard on doors.

Unexplained sounds and the breaking of glass have vexed those in the Ludlam house for years, and some guests have suspected that the building, rich in history and lore, just may be haunted.

"One guest came down for breakfast one morning," Ann Thurlow says, "and simply asked if the house was haunted. She said she detected a chilling sensation overnight, and knew that there was some sort of presence in the room with her."

So, who could be haunting the house?

The possibilities are tantalizing.

The Ludlam family extended over the generations has had its share of fascinating folks. There is the acceptance that Edgar Allan Poe's lyrical Annabel Lee was indeed a granddaughter of Henry Ludlam. She was a child and Poe was a child (to para-phrase the poet) in a kingdom by the sea, and although many Poe scholars believe Poe's tragic childhood love of "many and many a year ago" was fictional, and actually inspired by his thirteen year-old cousin and wife, Virginia, the Ludlam connection is intriguing.

One Ludlam who has a deeper etching in history is Jonathan Ludlam, who had been variously referred to as Henry Ludlam's son and grandson.

Ann Thurlow theorizes that Jonathan was the lawyer's son, but joins the legion of Ludlam investigators who are bemused by his exact place in the annals of Cape May's social register.

Some say Jonathan was a pirate, others claim he was a prince.

Much of Jonathan Ludlam's life story trails off into a cloud of historical oblivion. What is known about him, though, is that he (in the words of one writer) enjoyed a "cavalier" life at sea.

More correctly, it appears that most of his life "at sea" was really "on the bay." It was on the nearby Delaware Bay that Jonathan made his mark, so to speak.

While some accounts claim that Ludlam was one of several self-styled Delaware Bay freebooters who waylayed merchant sailors and claimed their cargo as his own, others maintain that he was a decorated, benevolent seaman.

There is evidence that he was once rewarded for bravery when he saved the crew of a schooner.

And, although even at his worst, Jonathan was credited with noble acts. Ann Thurlow recalls one report that after boarding a cargo boat on the bay and overpowering its crew, Ludlam brought them back to his Dennisville house and wined and dined them until he returned them to their plundered vessel.

Some say Jonathan Ludlam associated with the very meanest of the mean during the piracy days around Cape May. There are references to his being a slave runner and whiskey "importer," and some seemingly wild speculation holds that the multi-million dollar treasure of the ill-fated DeBraak may have been spirited away at one time by Ludlam and his men and actually buried somewhere on the sprawling Ludlam holdings in Cape May County.

If nothing else, the legend of Jonathan Ludlam is colorful and his legacy helps spice the history of the area.

What's more, it is said that Jonathan's ghost may very well inhabit the Ludlam House of Dennisville.

Ann Thurlow: "I have seen things go by. It's not a person, it's not anything I can describe. It looks like, well, like dashes, or like a wave. It passes by me and passes by quickly, and then it's gone."

Ann may fumble for words to describe her own feelings in her own inn, but others who have spent time there have more profound explanations and descriptions.

A handful of guests have claimed to have brushes with the spirits of Ludlam House. One person came down from their room for breakfast and calmly announced that they detected a "chilling sensation" the previous night in their rooms, felt that someone was in the room with them, and asked the Thurlows if the place was haunted.

Is it haunted? Ann Thurlow says the evidence is too heavily weighted on the affirmative to deny it. "In any case," she asserts, "I feel very protected here. I know that whatever might be in here will never do me or anyone else any harm. As for me, I feel that I am supposed to be here, if you know what I mean."

Of those who have reported to sense the presence of one or more ghosts in the inn, the most memorable was a woman who claimed to be a psychic.

She came to "read" the house and immediately discovered, through her psychic skills, the strong energy of two spirits. One, she said, was a tall, bearded man, seated in a chair. The other was a woman, whose disembodied wraith was making candles in one of the rooms. Their names, she claimed, were Jonathan and Rachel.

Even Ann Thurlow's mother once revealed an incident that led her to believe that not only mortals walk the pegged floorboards of the Ludlam House. "A couple of weeks ago," she said, "I was here and one night I woke up and I looked at the bottom of my bed and there was a child laying there. I thought, oh, I must be dreaming. But I know I wasn't."

The aforementioned psychic also claimed that the low, eerie crying of a baby could be heard from time to time in the house.

There could be another ghost in the house, if the testimony of another visitor is added to the others.

Ann Thurlow says the visitor came to the inn and asked if he could walk through it. He said he had lived there many years before.

"As he went into one of the upstairs rooms," Ann says, "he said 'you know, that's where I saw the ghost!' He said it was a spirit from the early 1900s, and was a woman. He said she had her hair pulled back, it was brown, and she was wearing a long, blue dress with little flowers on it.

"He said he saw her only once, and she never spoke a word."

Whoever or whatever it is that causes the noises in the night, the icy chills in August, and the apparitions in the Henry Ludlam House will likely always remain a mystery.

A SCARY NIGHT AT SEA

Commercial fisherman Dick Hess, of Goshen, Cape May County, has been going to sea in search of its bounty for more than twenty-five years. He is familiar with the lore of the seagoing individual, and aware of the long list of superstitions and traditions that are part of a sailor's very being.

He is doubtlessly familiar with legends such as the "Flying Dutchman," the phantom ship that is said to ply the seven seas; the "Sea Witch," which lurks around the Delaware Breakwater and guards the treasures of ancient wrecks and the other legends that have been told and retold by the mariners who set out in voyages to the farthest reaches of the world's oceans or to the rich fishing banks off Cape May.

Never in his wildest dreams did he expect to be a part of a bizarre episode that has become his own "Flying Dutchman."

The mid-October night was clear and calm back in 1978. The sky was awash with beads of light and the sea sloshed against the side of the 85-foot scallop boat, "Cayman."

The sturdy vessel was bound from Virginia to Cape May to "pack out," and Dick stood the night watch along with a shipmate named Jackie Hall. The captain and other crewmen were below decks, asleep.

All was quiet, and the two men on the weather deck were admiring the solitude of the evening and the particularly star-spangled sky.

In an instant, a bright light came out of nowhere and slashed across the sparkling overhead vista. At first glance, it appeared to be nothing more than a brilliant and alarmingly close "shooting star," a fairly common sight on clear nights at sea.

But Dick and Jackie watched intently as the white light seemed to hover a distance away. They paid particular attention as it sped toward the Cayman at a speed the two men estimated at forty to fifty miles per hour.

Neither had ever seen anything like it in their many years at sea. All sorts of thoughts crossed their minds in the moments they gazed upon the blazing pinpoint.

They quickly reasoned that it was not a shooting star, nor was it an aircraft, or approaching boat. Their best description was that it looked like a huge floodlight or spotlight, aimed at their vessel and approaching rapidly.

Fleeting thoughts in their minds recollected the tales of sea monsters and phantom ships, even Unidentified Flying Objects. Both men, however, considered themselves to be too pragmatic to accept any of these possibilities.

Still, there was no rational explanation.

Dick left the wheelhouse, where both men had been, for a closer look from the bow. As the boat and light got closer, he noticed something remarkable.

The light was actually beneath the surface of the water. It was shining up from the sea. As the boat approached the light, both men shuddered. Perhaps it really was an aircraft that crashed into the ocean and was wallowing just beneath the waves. But never, throughout the course of the event, was there any noise, any wake, or any recognizable form to the light.

The light seemed to be attracted to the boat and continued to come closer until it shined up from under the hull of the Cayman. It seemed to be sizing up the vessel as it paused for a few seconds and shot away from it quickly, disappearing into the depths.

Again, no wake, no sound. The show was over. There never was enough time to wake the captain and crewmembers, and while the brief but memorable event was unfolding, neither Dick Hess or Jackie Hall could release themselves from the grip of the hypotizing and baffling light.

They told their tale to a skeptical crew. They didn't care about the ridicule they may have received because both sober and drug-free men knew exactly what they had seen and knew no one would ever really understand.

To this day, Dick Hess marvels at whatever might have happened that night off Cape May. He has allowed any even remotely plausible explanation to pass through his reasoning. The actions of the light were too radical for it to be a downed aircraft. It moved too rapidly to be a submarine—besides, both men clearly saw it drop from the sky into the sea.

They can only figure, reluctantly as they may, that it really was a UFO. It's not an explanation they're comfortable with, but it's the best they can do.

THE BUNKER

"I never really knew what I saw that night," the young man said while puffing incessantly on another cigarette.

It was a cold night in Wilmington when the researchers met with Bill and Karen Dodson, who were to tell the story of their encounter with the unknown on the beach of Cape May Point in the autumn of 1987.

Their names are fictitious, at their own request. Their story is baffling, and just might change the way you think about a quiet walk along the beach as the sun sinks across the bay.

"We love Cape May," Karen asserted. "We loved it then and we love it now, even though we had that strange experience down near that old bunker on the beach.

"I feel odd just sitting here talking to you," she continued. "We have told this story to a few of our friends and to be very frank, most of them laugh it off and think we are crazy. You probably will, too. Heck, we probably will think we're crazy once we read it in print."

Karen, a lovely soft-spoken redhead who has spent, to her best estimation, portions of at least ten of her twenty-six summers on Cape May vacations, said that her "very favorite thing" at the shore was a stroll in the sand at sunset.

"I would alternate the beaches," she chuckled. I really loved Higbee Beach. I heard all the stories about how one of Captain Kidd's pirates was buried there to guard treasure, and how old man Higbee's ghost might haunt the place. Someone even told me that the old guy was buried face down so he could meet the Devil. I must say that I was fascinated by those kinds of stories as a little girl, but I cannot say that I ever really believed in ghosts at all. But even after what happened to Billy and I last fall, I still love to walk the beach, any beach, especially around sunset and after."

So what happened on that evening? Bill started first: "Well," he said, "Karen and I were renting a place down there, as we have during the last five or six summers. We took our nightly walk down to the beach. We had done this many, many times. Even in cold or rainy weather, there we'd be, walking up and over the dunes near the lighthouse and then up and down the beach. I'm not a romantic person, and I guess this was pretty romantic, when I think about it."

Karen giggled as her husband fumbled through the issue of romance. "Bull," she directed to her mate, "you know you loved every minute of it!" They both laughed and clasped each other's hands.

"Anyway," Bill continued after taking a deep breath as if to bolster himself for the statement that was to follow, "I think it was around 7:30 that particular night when we hiked onto the beach. There were a lot of clouds in the sky and sunset was coming quickly. It was kind of twilight.

"That night, Karen and I somehow decided to head over toward the old concrete bunker that sits out in the surf. I don't know why we went that direction, we just did.

"I must say that it was a little weird that night. The clouds looked like storm clouds and the sky was turning very gray. Everything stated to get sort of purplish then, if you know what I mean.

"It was very obvious, as we walked toward the old bunker, that there was somebody else on it. You know, there is a catwalk up to it and a deck on top of it. Well, we could see three or four people on top of it, and way out as far away as we were at the time, we could hear them talking. It sounded like a group of men, laughing and shooting the breeze."

Karen said she saw the flicker of what she thought was a match or lighter come from the bunker top, and mentioned it to Bill. "To be honest," she said, "I was a little suspicious, or cautious. Maybe they were up to no good, and maybe it was best if we avoided them and the bunker and walked in the other direction. Bill said I was nuts, so we kept going in that direction."

Bill said he stared at the bunker almost all the while the couple walked the relatively short walk to the monstrous bulk of concrete that served as a lookout post during the second world war.

"I'm fascinated by the thing," he admitted. "I can't help but think of what it must have been like in those days. Guys were actually stationed on that thing, I guess, and there really was a threat of Nazi submarines coming close to Cape May. I read in your other book about shipwrecks down there that they think a German sub might even have come up the bay. Well, I treat that old bunker as some kind of wartime relic in my mind.

"I was looking at it as we walked, except for a couple of times I had to look where I was walking or when Karen distracted me. I even looked at those men on top of the bunker and I know for certain that they were there. There was no doubt in my mind or Karen's mind that we saw and heard them."

Karen agreed. "Oh, yes," she concurred, "they were there. We couldn't make out any faces or dress, and we couldn't understand what they were saying, but they were definitely there. And, at the time, we didn't think much of it.

"We got closer to the bunker," Karen continued, "and the men were still there. We hesitated a little and decided we wouldn't go any farther, or walk onto the bunker. Really, we never intended to, but the men scared us away a little. I mean, there was nothing frightening about them at all. In fact, from where we were at that point, we couldn't even see them any longer.

"We heard them, though. Again, we couldn't pinpoint anything they were saying, but every once in a while we heard some recognizable words and some loud bursts of laughter."

Bill confirmed Karen's remarks. "I know we both picked up on a couple of loud cuss words and we both thought we heard one of the guys mention the Yankees, the baseball team."

There was never a notion of anything ghostly that may have been happening at the time. Neither Bill nor Karen had any thoughts of the supernatural, and there was no reason for them to have any.

That all changed very quickly after the couple lingered near the catwalk that led to the bunker's observation deck.

"We didn't really plan on it," Bill said. "We were just standing around, in fact, I think we sat down on a mound of sand. I remember that I was sifting through the sand and just watching the clouds forming over the sun."

Karen remembered that yes, the two did "plop down on the sand," and as they sat there, strange things started to happen. "I don't know, but for some reason I noticed that the laughter and the talking on the bunker had stopped. I really heard the moment when it stopped. I was sort of preoccupied by it and remember that there was a sudden end to all the noise. I kept it to myself, and I really had no reason to say anything to Bill about it. Again, the idea of ghosts or anything like them was the farthest from our minds.

"Everything was quiet, and just a second or two after the chatter on the bunker ended, I looked over to it. I clearly saw the bunker, the catwalk, and it wasn't very far away.

"It was getting darker, but there still was plenty of light enough to make out details on the bunker's walls and things like that. Like I said, I didn't tell Bill that I thought it was strange how the laughter and conversation ended so quickly. Then, though, he nudged me and asked me if I thought it got real quiet all of a sudden."

Bill said he heard the end of the conversation coming from the bunker, too. At first, he thought nothing of it. "It did stick in my mind for a few seconds," he said. "I asked Karen about it, just a couple of seconds after it happened. We both then looked over toward the bunker and expected to see whoever it was up on the deck come across the catwalk. We waited several minutes and there was nobody and no noise.

"I know for an absolute fact that nobody left that bunker deck," Karen said. "Then, Bill just happened to stand up and walk up higher onto the dune to look across the deck of the bunker. He whispered down to me 'Karen, you're not going to believe this, but there's nobody on that deck,' or something like that."

Bill continued. "She's right. I could see very clearly onto the deck, and as a matter of fact the last rays of the sun sort of shined down between the clouds and made the surface of the deck very clear. There was nobody there."

At that point, both Bill and Karen thought something was a bit out of kilter. They knew what they saw and heard. Between the two of them, they never really let the bunker out of their sight. Still, the forms they saw on top of it disappeared and the sounds they heard coming from it ceased abruptly. They were confused, and, by their own admission, finally somewhat frightened.

"You know," Karen said, "I still don't say I believe in ghosts, and maybe this little experience we had had nothing to do with ghosts. I mean, we're not saying that that bunker is haunted or anything, but we don't really know what else to think or how else to explain what happened that night. We just walked away from the bunker after what happened, across the highest part of the dune we could walk on, and kept looking at the bunker all the way. Nobody ever left it, there was nobody on it, and all the noise we heard had stopped. I guess we'll never figure it out."

ABOUT THE AUTHORS

This is the fifth collaboration of David J. Seibold and Charles J. Adams III.

Seibold, an avid fisherman and scuba diver, resides in Barnegat Light, N.J. and Wyomissing Hills, Pa.

A graduate of Penn State University, Seibold is a member of the Barnegat Light Scuba and Rescue Team and operates his own charter boat out of Barnegat Light.

He is a former commodore of the Rajah Temple Yacht Club and served as a company commander in the Vietnam War after being commissioned in the U.S. Army Signal Corps.

Seibold is also employed as an account executive at WEEU Broadcasting Co. He is a member of many civic and social organizations, and the Steamship Historical Society.

Charles J. Adams III has written eight books, and has published numerous articles, songs and stories.

He is the morning radio personality at WEEU radio, Reading, Pa., and is the Reading Sunday Eagle newspaper's chief travel correspondent. His "Travels With Charlie" column appears regularly in the Eagle.

Adams is president of the Reading Public Library board of trustees, and also sits on the executive council and editorial board of the Historical Society of Berks County, Pa. He is also a member of the board of directors of the

Penn State Alumni Society of the Berks Campus and is active in many civic and social organizations.

Seibold and Adams are currently researching another book on shipwrecks and legends of the northern New Jersey coast.

ABOUT THE ARTIST

The cover artwork and other incidental art in this book is the work of Linda Perno Dotter.

Mrs. Dotter, of Freehold and Barnegat Light N.J., attended the Newark School of Fine and Industrial Arts, and has exhibited her art numerous times in her native northern New Jersey.

She divides her time between her many freelance art assignments and caring for her husband, Joseph, and their four children.

Her artistic endeavors were also featured in Seibold and Adams' previous books, "Shipwrecks and Legends 'round Cape May," and "Shipwrecks Off Ocean City."

CAPE MAY GHOST STORIES

PHOTO GALLERY

The Washington Inn in Cape May is said to be haunted by a ghost the owners have named "Elizabeth." (Photo by Charles J. Adams III)

Strange events on the old World War II bunker were noticed by a Delaware couple while they walked along this stretch of beach. (Photo by Charles J. Adams III)

The ghostly figure of a young woman was spotted on this bed in the Wicker Room of the Windward House. (Photo by Charles J. Adams III)

"The Light of Asia" wooden elephant once stood on a Cape May beach and was reportedly haunted. (Photo courtesy of Sarah (Sue) Leaming)

The stately "Colvmns-by-the Sea" inn has had it share of ghostly events. (Photo by Charles J. Adams III)

The antique baby carriage in this photo reportedly moves with no human aid across a hall of the Colvmns-by the Sea's second floor. (Photo by David J. Seibold)

A view of the "crying" wall at the Colvmns-by-the-Sea inn on the Cape May beachfront. (Photo by David J. Seibold)

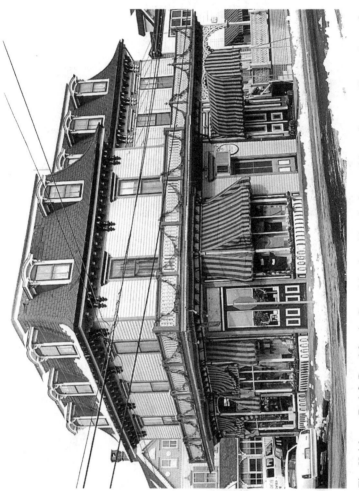

The Heirloom Bed & Breakfast in Cape May is said to be haunted by at least one benevolent ghost. (Photo by Charles J. Adams III)

The third floor "Plum Room" of the Heirloom Bed & Breakfast has been the site of ghostly activity. (Photo by David J. Seibold)

A vintage photograph of "the haunted book store," Keltie's, when it was Knerr's Dry Goods shop. (Photo courtesy of Sarah (Sue) Leaming)

Ghostly forms and shuffling books have been witnessed at Keltie's News and Books in Cape May. (Photo by Charles J. Adams III)

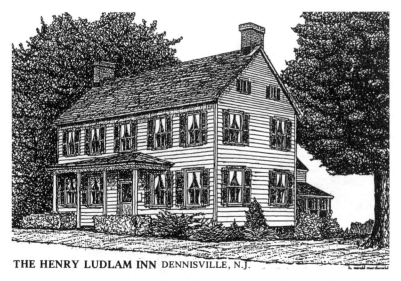

THE HENRY LUDLAM INN DENNISVILLE, N.J.

It is believed that a former resident of what is now the Henry Ludlam Inn at Dennisville may never have left the place. (Photo courtesy of Ann Thurlow)

At least one person has reported sighting a ghost in the old John Holmes House, which now serves as headquarters for the Cape May Historical Society. (Photo by Charles J. Adams III)

85

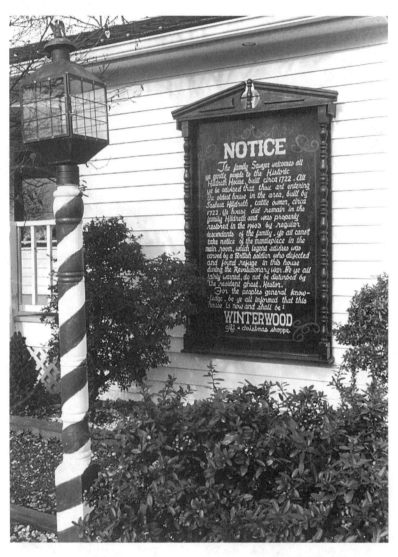

A sign on the outside wall of Winterwood in Rio Grande warns all who approach of the ghost that walks the halls inside. (Photo by Charles J. Adams III)

The mantelpiece in Winterwood was carved by a British soldier who defected during the Revolution and took refuge in the old house. There have been several ghost sightings in the building, which serve as a Christmas shop. (Photo by Charles J. Adams III)

The former Hildreth House, now the Christmas shop called Winterwood, is supposedly haunted by the ghost of a woman. (Photo by Charles J. Adams III)

View at Lily Lake, Rustic Bridge, Cape May Point, N. J.

A turn-of-the-century view of Lake Lily, the site of many legends and eerie occurrences at Cape May Point.

The Windward House on Jackson Street in Cape May has been the scene of supernatural occurrences. (Photo by Charles J. Adams III)

Could it be that a ghostly crew still mans this World War II lookout bunker on Cape May? (Photo by Charles J. Adams III)

Co-author David J. Seibold gazes out to sea at a site where the ghost of a young boy is said to walk the beach of the Cape May. (Photo by Charles J. Adams III)

EXETER HOUSE BOOKS
CURRENT AVAILABLE TITLES

Read more about the shore in these other books by David J. Seibold and Charles J. Adams III:

SHIPWRECKS AND LEGENDS 'ROUND CAPE
   MAY (1987)
SHIPWRECKS OFF OCEAN CITY (1986)
LEGENDS OF LONG BEACH ISLAND (1985)
SHIPWRECKS NEAR BARNEGAT INLET (1984)

A FINAL WORD

The authors of Cape May Ghost Stories are continuing in their quest to research and record any and all stories of the supernatural from Cape May, and, in fact any area along the New Jersey shore.

If you have any experiences you would be willing to discuss with them for possible future publication, please write to them at Exeter House Books, P.O. Box 91, Barnegat Light, N.J. 08006

Please include you name, address and telephone number, and a brief summary of your story. All identities and addresses will be held in the strictest confidence, and complete anonymity is guaranteed.